Soldier's Next Journey

Heather Morris

ACKNOWLEDGMENTS

As we near the end of our Colvin series, I want to make sure my readers know just how much they mean to me. I have enjoyed taking you all on the journey through the Blake family's lives and couldn't have done it without you. My family and friends have been so patient and supportive and they're a true blessing.

I want a big thank you to go to Kristi Estes for being the one who got the words from my brain to the computer. I was struggling getting the time and energy to type for hours on end to get the story down on paper but she was more than willing to help get this book out there! She was a life saver for this one and I can't thank her enough!

THE COLVIN SERIES BOOK LIST
(SO FAR)

Book 1- Down to the Creek- Aiden & Karlie

Book 2- Nursery in Bloom- Austin & Leah

Book 3- Third Time's a Charm- Audrey & Maysen

Book 4- Life's a Gamble- Aaron & Amie

Book 5- Soldier's Next Journey- Jonathan & Lizzie

"Today's the day right?" I hear Tarley say from the doorway. I've been with him since we first enlisted and he's more like a brother than a friend. Pain in the butt for sure but he always has my back.

I look up and try to smile while my insides are doing flips. I'm not real sure how I'm supposed to feel today. This is a day that I never dreamed I would be going through.

Today I meet my little girl for the first time. My little girl. Unbelievable. I just found out a few days ago that I have a two year old little girl that I didn't have a clue existed. Her mom passed away from cancer a couple of weeks ago and left a letter telling me about Arianna.

I had just returned from Iraq to Fort Bragg when I received Marianna's letter. To say I was shocked wouldn't suffice. I was blown away and my whole world was turned upside down. Having children wasn't something I thought I would do for a long time since I've been in the Army. For one, I don't even have a girlfriend or even a woman that's in my life other than my mother and sister.

"I still can't believe I'm going to meet my little girl. Mine. I feel like I'm in some parallel universe right now."

Tarley walks over and puts his arm on my shoulder and says with a very mischievous grin, "Dude if you need backup I would be more than happy to go with you."

"You're incorrigible. I told you she's off limits to you man. Forget it. I haven't even seen her. She could be hideous." I don't believe a word that I said because she sounded amazing. But he doesn't need to know that.

"Hey I told you I'd always have your back." Another grin.

"This sounds like a hardship for you. I'll see you when I get back. I'm going to be late if I don't leave now." I take a deep breath.

"Here are the keys to my pickup. Be careful with her please. She's all I've got man."

I take the keys from him and smile, "Thanks man I appreciate it."

"I mean it, be careful. You scratch her I'll kick your butt. Got it?"

"Got it. Later." I sigh and walk to his pickup still unable to wrap my head around the thought that I'm going to see a little girl that shares my DNA. Unbelievable.

***

As Arianna and I sit in the car at her favorite park I'm having trouble keeping the butterflies in my stomach contained. They're doing circus acts and running marathons inside. My hands are shaking and I'm sweating. This is ridiculous.

What if Jonathan wants to take Arianna away from me? What if he decides she's better with me? What would Marianna really want?

Ahhhhh these darn questions won't stop swirling around in my brain. I don't think I've slept much since I got the first call from Jonathan. And Arianna knows something's up because she keeps asking me why I'm sad. Not sad really, just nervous beyond anything I've ever felt before.

Please dear Lord let me say the right things at the right times. Please help me to keep my nerves hidden when I meet this guy. Please help me to keep Arianna's best interests at the fore front.

I take one more deep breath and decide it's now or never.

"Ready to go on the slide Arianna?" I get out and open her door. She's wriggling and excited to go to the park. She has no clue that

2

her life is about to change too. If only I could be that excited about this whole situation.

Yes, he sounded so sweet and sexy on the phone, but this is NOT about me and my hormones. It's about Arianna and her father. Wow father.

"Swings swings swings!" She yells as I set her down on the grass. Just as I do she runs to the swing set and tries to get in one.

"Patience my dear I have to put our stuff down first." I walk over to the nearby picnic table and set my purse and her diaper bag down.

"Swing swing!" I walk over and put her into the baby swing and start to push her backwards. The higher she gets the bigger her smile gets.

Seeing that smile is the best medicine after the past couple of weeks we've had since my sister, her mother, passed away. Arianna has definitely bounced back faster than I have but having her does make it a little easier. I vowed to Marianna that I would always take care of her little girl as if she were my own. And now I have to protect her or whatever from the man that knocked my sister up before disappearing.

Now Lizzie you can't say that. Marianna never even told him she was pregnant. He hasn't known he was a father. Until now. Oh my goodness how am I going to do this? Maybe if I get her in the car right now we can be gone before he gets here. I can't do this.

I start to lift Arianna out of the swing when I hear someone come up behind me and then I hear that somewhat familiar male voice. Oh crap here it goes ready or not.

"Are you Lizzie?" I turn and about drop Arianna out of the swing. This man standing in front of us with a pink teddy bear is the picture of hot male soldier that every woman's fantasies are made of. Oh my goodness.

"Um y-y-yes I'm Lizzie. Are you J-j-jonathan?" I stutter. I must look and sound like the biggest idiot.

"Yes, it's so good to finally put a face to the name. And voice."

"Likewise. Did you have trouble finding the place?" I set Arianna back in the seat and nudge the swing to move again then step between her and this man that helped bring her into the world.

"No the GPS did the work. Um I really don't know how this is supposed to go. Please forgive me for being so nervous. This is for Arianna." He hands me the bear and wipes his palms on the legs of his jeans. He is nervous. A part of me feels sorry for the guy.

"Me neither. Um maybe we can just go slow? She doesn't know who you are or anything about you. Well I guess I don't either. Something tells me Marianna didn't either." I say and step aside so that he can come closer to where Arianna is swinging happily.

"She loves to swing doesn't she?"

"Yes. The higher the happier she gets. Not sure where she gets that but it makes her happiest."

"I would have to say from me. I love anything fast and dangerous. I guess that's why I've been in the Army for so long. The rush and sense of duty makes me happy."

"How long have you been in the Army?"

"About six years."

"Thank you for your service and keeping us safe."

"Of course. What about you? What do you do?"

"I'm an artist. I paint whatever my clients want me to paint."

4

"You don't sound happy about that. Almost bored."

"No, I just don't really get to paint what I want to anymore, just what others want. But I get paid really well so I can't complain."

"That's awesome. Not everyone gets to do what they love."

"Are you done with the Army or do you have to go back overseas?" Not real sure why I asked that but I guess I do need to know.

"Um I honestly don't know yet. We just got back so I have some time to figure it out but now with all this I have a lot of other stuff to consider." He motions to Arianna.

"I understand. When Marianna got sick and decided I would take her place, I had to really think hard about where I would go from there too. She was sick for so long that I've been filling the mom role a lot longer than she did."

"Was she peaceful at the end? I'm sorry that's personal." He says shaking his head.

"No, it's okay you have every right to ask questions. I'm sorry you didn't know about Arianna until now." I turn and lift her out of the swing and hold her close kissing the sweet little forehead in front of me.

"She is so beautiful and looks so much like my sister Karlie." He lifts his hand to touch Arianna's hand but withdraws it before he connects with it.

"It's okay you can touch her. She won't bite."

"I am so out of my league here. I've never even seen my niece and now I'm a father. This is all so hard to believe."

"I understand fully. Let's take it slow."

"I would appreciate that. I don't want to say or do the wrong thing here."

"Well, Jonathan this is Arianna. Arianna this is my, my, my friend Jonathan. Can you say hi?" She looks up at Jonathan and smiles that cute little baby face smile with slobber running out of her mouth.

"Hello." She says in that baby gibberish she's starting to lose.

"Hello sweet girl. You sure are a happy little one aren't you?" This time he reaches out his finger and as soon as he does she wraps her fingers around it. He looks a little surprised and sucks in a quick breath then smiles.

"Well that's a good sign. We've been working on being nice to everyone but she normally doesn't let anyone touch her. She shies away from everyone and buries her face into my neck." She really isn't acting like she usually does. That makes me a little more nervous because she instinctively likes this guy. Does she know he's her dad? Surely not.

"She can't know can she?" He asks with a look of complete terror on his face.

"Know that you're her dad? I doubt it."

"Dada?" We both jump when we hear Arianna say that word and pulls Jonathan's finger into her mouth. He pulls it away quickly and steps back.

"Um, Arianna are you ready for the slide?" I try to distract her from that question. It's a little soon for that. He pulled away from her so quickly it was like he had gotten burned.

"Swide!" She squirms until I set her down on the ground where she toddles off towards the slide.

"I'm sorry about that. She heard me say dad but I don't think she knows anything. And we won't tell her until you're ready if that's what you decide you want."

2

Decide that I want that? Is she crazy? I may not have known this little girl existed but how can I turn my back on her and act like I don't know about her now? What kind of a person does that? I had an amazing father and can't imagine leaving this girl parentless.

But I know nothing about being a father. I've never even held a little person before. How the heck do I go from me to father? I have to get home to talk to mom and Karlie. Even Aiden could help me out in this department.

"I don't know where this is all going to take us but I do want you to know that I won't turn my back on my own flesh and blood. Family is everything to me." I say while running my fingers through what little hair I have.

"Tell me all about them and you." Lizzie walks to the nearby park bench and sits while motioning for me to join her.

"Well, I grew up in a small town in Oklahoma named Colvin. I have a little sister named Karlie. My parents' names are Gene and Ella Mae. My father passed away but my mom and sister still live there. Karlie married her high school sweetheart Aiden Blake and they have a little girl a bit younger than Arianna named Aleah. Um, my sister is a photographer and mom owns a bakery shop downtown."

"Wow. They sound wonderful. Just one sibling too huh? Marianna and I grew up with only each other too. We were very close and when we lost Mama to cancer it hit Marianna a lot harder than me. I had always been the artsy one and Marianna was the caregiver. She took care of Mama all the way until the end. Our father was never around much and he completely split when he found out Mama was pregnant with Marianna. Two kids were just too much for him I guess."

"That's terrible. I grew up with amazing parents. I guess that's why I feel so strong about doing the right thing for Arianna."

"You aren't obligated to be here you know. I'll gladly take care of her for the rest of her life without you."

"I don't feel obligated exactly. You say it like it's a bad thing. I don't feel like that."

"I'm sorry I just assumed. Hunky soldier just home from Iraq. Figured you would want to get back home and back to your life. And maybe girlfriend or wife?"

"Neither of those. Hunky huh?" I smile and see the red creep up on Lizzie's face.

"Well who can resist the charms of a soldier? Anyway, have you told your family about Arianna yet?"

"No. That's something I need to do in person not over the phone. I wanted to meet her first and see how it felt."

"And how did it feel exactly?"

"I won't lie, it feels weird. I feel a pull to her but I also know we are strangers."

"True. But you do know you don't have to make any quick decisions here. She's got her whole life here and she's been fine without you so far."

"Ouch."

"I'm so sorry I didn't mean that to come out so rude. I'm simply saying that we don't have to jump into anything. We have time to get used to things and take it one step at a time."

"I appreciate that. I was thinking I'd go home tomorrow and let everyone know the good news."

"What do you think they're going to say?"

"My mother is going to tan my hide." I smile and lean my head back laughing. It feels good to laugh and relieve some tension.

"Is she going to accept Arianna or never want to see her?"

"She's going to be tough to keep away from Arianna."

"Oh boy. One of those." She smiles that amazing smile and I see a little dimple on the right side of her mouth. I have to try hard to keep from reaching over and touching it.

What the heck is wrong with me? Am I just that emotionally messed up right now or is it that she's the first woman I've been around for a long time? Well at least one not in a uniform.

"She's an amazing person I promise. She's so full of love and tenderness you'll not be able to keep yourself from falling in love with her."

"Ah ok. Arianna do you wanna go down the slide again?" She looks over at Arianna who has been sitting at our feet playing in the sand.

Arianna looks up with a toothy and slobbery grin and lifts her arms up. Lizzie stands up and bends down to pick her up but Arianna shakes her head and points over to me. I look at Lizzie with a confused look and she only smiles.

"She wants you to take her on the slide. Are you up for that? Or too soon?"

"Do I just hold her on my lap or what?" I stand up rubbing my hands on my jeans again. I instantly went full of nerves again. How can such a little human freak me out so quickly even after I've been on four tours in the Army?

"Yes, pick her up and climb the stairs with her. Then sit down with her on your lap and go down the big slide."

"Um I think I can handle that." I can't help but keep the smile off my face. The thought of holding Arianna makes me a little giddy inside. This must be the parental instincts kicking in? Wow.

"Jonathan will take you down the slide and I'll be right at the bottom waiting for you okay?" Lizzie says to her as I lean down to pick her up. She's smiling that huge smile still and it makes my heart catch.

"Ready squirt?" I pick her up and she immediately lays her head on my shoulder making that feeling inside me get even bigger.

"Wow she really likes you already. Very uncommon for her." The crease between Lizzie's eye brows is getting more pronounced. I don't think she knows what to think here either.

"Let's go down this slide young lady. I don't think I've been down one since I was a little boy." I smile and think how bizarre this feels but also how good it feels.

I climb the stairs to the slide and when we get closer to the top I feel Arianna clench onto me tighter. I also strengthen my grip on her and position myself so I can slide us down.

"Are you ready squirt?" I ask right before Arianna turns and kisses my cheek. Holy goodness I'm at a loss now! This sweet little person is going to hook me long before I'm ready.

Or maybe I am ready?

"Here we go." I push off and down we slide around and around until the sight of a beautiful woman comes into view. She's standing at the bottom with a grin the size of Texas and her arms open wide for Arianna. If I didn't know differently I would think this girl is her Mama instead of an aunt.

"Was that fun baby girl?" She says and takes Arianna from my arms. I immediately feel empty without her little body clamped on my arms. This is bizarre. There's that word again. Bizarre. I don't know what other word to use to explain this whole situation and these feelings I have bubbling up inside.

I watch as Lizzie twirls Arianna around in a circle making the little girl giggle loudly. I can't help but smile at the sight they make. Wow there's that feeling again. Maybe I'm getting sick. Maybe. Yea right.

"She loves that doesn't she?" I ask and touch the back of Arianna's head. What did I do that for? I did it before I even thought about it. Lizzie is looking at me strange too like she's hearing what's going on in my head.

"Well, I guess I had better get going. I've got to pack and get to the airport early tomorrow. Don't forget the teddy bear that I got you." I hand Arianna the bear and step back wanting to get some clarity. These two females have my emotions and head so jumbled up I'm not sure if I know my name.

"I can understand that. Thank you for coming to such a non-personal place to meet her for the first time."

"To meet you both for the first time." I smile at her wanting to calm her down just as much as myself.

"It was very nice to meet you Jonathan. Have a safe trip." She tries to shake my hand but I pull her in for a hug instead. That just didn't feel right shaking her hand. We're going to be around each other a lot now so we need to be friends. Right?

"Um ok well I'll talk to you soon. Bye Arianna. It was so nice playing with you today. Be good for Lizzie okay? Bye Lizzie." I say and once again touch Arianna's head. That's becoming way too familiar. Hmmm. Maybe I CAN do this.

***

He hugged us. Why did he hug us? That was so weird. And nice. What am I saying?

"Bye Jonathan. Have a safe trip. You know where to find us." I wave goodbye as he gets in his pickup. A part of me feels sad that he's leaving and I really don't know when or if I'll ever see him again. But then the other feels relieved because he left without Arianna.

"Dada dada." Arianna says and points to his retreating vehicle and then the pink teddy bear he left behind.

I gasp and wrap my arms around her tighter. She can't possibly know can she? Surely not.

"Are you ready to go home and have a snack? Maybe you should draw another picture for the fridge. Or we can play with your kitchen?" I say trying to distract her from the D word. Wow.

"Dada dada dada." Oh boy. What in the world do I do now?

I get her situated into her car seat and take a little breather outside my door before getting inside. I can do this. Marianna give me strength to do this. Ahhhhh.

"Okay let's go home and have some fun okay? Look out the window for some airplanes." Another shot at distraction. This time it worked.

"Air-pane air-pane!"

"Thank you Marianna." I mumble under my breath and sigh a deep cleansing sigh before pulling out of our parking spot and driving towards home.

I wonder how long this will continue to be her home? My home. Our home. Oh boy this isn't going to be easy. What have you gotten me into baby sister?

5

"Jonathan you're home! I'm so glad to see you son!" My mom says as she runs towards me in the Tulsa airport. It's been so long since I've seen her and my insides turn to mush as I wrap her in my arms.

"Hey Mom. So good to be home."

"Your sister couldn't come because Aleah's naptime is about now and Aiden had a meeting at the AK so he couldn't keep her."

"No biggie. I'll see them later. That gives us a chance to catch up." Boy does she ever need to catch up. She's going to smack me I'm sure when she hears about Arianna.

"Yes we do. My son has been gone a long time. Are you home for good now?" I knew that question was coming.

"Mom, I'm not really sure about anything except I can't wait to get home."

"Got it. Let's go. The car is over this way." And I follow the most important woman in my life to her car. She's rattling on so quickly about Karlie and Aleah that I'm having a hard time keeping up. I smile knowing she's going to love Arianna just as much. Wow, I'm serious about being there for her aren't I? Of course I am, was there ever any doubt? Definitely not once I saw her in person.

I miss her actually. And her aunt. Oh my goodness I miss them? I just met them how can I already miss them? I don't know them!

"Jonathan, Earth to Jonathan! Where are you?" I look up and see Mom holding the trunk open for my bags looking confused.

"Sorry I was running a few things I have to do through my head." I hoist my stuff inside and grab the keys from her. "I'll drive."

"Figured you would."

I smile and get into the driver's seat.

"What's on your mind son? You look distracted."

"Mom I have to tell you something but I'm not sure how you're going to react."

"Please tell me you didn't enlist again!"

"No, not that. This is something life changing though."

"You're getting married? I didn't know you even had a girlfriend!"

"Um no. No girlfriend, no wedding. Sorry to disappoint you." I smile knowing how much Mom loves to plan weddings.

"Then what is it Jonathan? You're scaring your old mother here."

"Sorry. I don't know where to start."

"At the beginning would be good."

"Okay. Here goes. No smacking me while I'm behind the wheel."

"That's the reason you wanted to drive wasn't it?" She laughs and puts her arm on mine as a sign of support.

"I have a little girl named Arianna. I just found out about her earlier this week."

"What?!?! Did you say a daughter?"

"Yes. I got a letter soon after we returned to Post and it had a picture inside. I met her yesterday."

"Well, where is she? Why isn't she with you? Jonathan where is she?"

"She lives in Temple, North Carolina with her aunt Lizzie."

"She lives with her aunt? Where's her mother?"

"She passed away a few weeks ago from cancer. She left a letter for me if anything ever happened to her. That's why I just found out about Arianna."

"Oh how terrible Jonathan. You need to get that girl and bring her here so we can love her and give her a better life than she's had. You didn't know anything about her until now?"

I finish telling Mom the whole story and let her read Marianna's letter. There's so much to it that I couldn't possibly explain it all. I keep hearing her gasp as she's reading the letter but she remains silent.

"So you said you met them yesterday? What was she like? Was the aunt nice to you?"

"She looks just like Karlie but with dark hair. Lizzie was wonderful too. I think she's afraid of losing her. She loves her like she's her own child."

"So you're torn as to what to do aren't you?"

"Yes I am. I'm her father but she's the only family Arianna has known."

"Until now. She has a whole family here to love her too."

"Yes but can I take her away from what she knows and Lizzie."

"Maybe you should marry Lizzie and move them here. End of story."

"What?!?! You do realize I'm driving right? That's not something you say to someone trying to concentrate on driving! I can't just marry this girl. I just met her. Wow I can't believe you said that Mom." I shake my head to clear the shock away. Marry Lizzie? Is she crazy? Hmmm maybe that isn't as bad to think about. Shut up Jonathan that's insane!

4

"Hi Sylvia. How are you?" I should've known she'd call first thing today to find out how the meeting with Jonathan went.

"Good, thank you. Lizzie you know why I'm calling don't you?"

"Of course I do. Things went better than I expected them to."

"Why do you say better? Did he say he didn't want Arianna in his life?"

"Oh goodness no. I don't think he would ever do that to her."

"Then what has you so optimistic about this situation now?"

"He was great with her. He didn't push and was actually very nervous. The poor guy. When she took his finger and put it in her mouth I thought he was going to take off running." I laugh and hear Sylvia laugh too.

"Some men who have never been around babies before react a bit different don't they?"

"He recovered well and even took her down the slide. I think he was a little torn about leaving us there. I mean leaving Arianna there."

"You said us. Do you like this guy? Like as more than just the father of your niece?"

"Sylvia don't be ridiculous. I just met him and couldn't have any sort of thought like that." She doesn't need to know that I was attracted to Jonathan and have actually had thoughts about us raising Arianna together. No one needs to know that.

"Okay you just sounded strange. I'm glad things went well. When did he say he wanted to see her again?"

"He flew back to Oklahoma today where he's from. He wanted to tell his family about Arianna and would get in touch with me once he had. I don't really know where to go from here."

"Just go about your normal lives and wait for him to make a move. If you think he's a good guy then don't expect the worst and stay positive."

"I'll try. Believe me it was hard to see him with her and then she called him dada and we both freaked out. I had just said the word not that anyone told her he was her dad. It was just so weird."

"Wow she's perceptive. She's never had a dad so I highly doubt she actually knows what that means. Don't worry about it. Like I said, normal lives until he makes another move. If you need me just call. You have my cell. Talk to you later."

"Bye Sylvia thank you so much for calling."

I wish it were as easy as Sylvia thinks it will be to go back to our normal lives. What's normal now that we know Jonathan and he knows us? Thanks a lot Marianna. This is a big mess. I pray I can do what it is you would want and what's best for Arianna.

***

"Jonathan!!!!!" I hear a woman squeal from behind me when I'm getting out of mom's car in her driveway. I turn to see the most beautiful red head running towards me smiling that gorgeous smile she has always had.

"Hey Karlie! I wondered if you'd be here." I say as I accept her into my open arms and wrap them around her. I have missed these two so much and I hadn't realized it until I was hugging each of them so tightly.

"I have missed you so much big brother!"

"I've missed you too sis. Where's that gorgeous niece of mine?" I look behind her to see Aiden walking up carrying the most adorable little girl I have ever seen. Well, except for my own I think to myself. "Hey Aiden!"

"Hey Jonathan, how ya been? Long time no see." Aiden says and gives me a quick hug. Another hug. Too bad we're to the end of my welcoming committee because I could get used to this. I smile and look at my niece.

"Jonathan I'd like you to meet my daughter. This is your niece Aleah. Baby, this is Uncle Jonathan." Karlie takes the baby from Aiden and hands her to me. This would feel so strange to me if I hadn't have already held my own little person just yesterday.

"Well hello there Aleah. Aren't you just beautiful like your mama." I look at her and think that she doesn't look near as much like Karlie as Arianna does. Aleah got enough of the Blake genes in her that she might look a lot more like Aiden. Hard to tell at this age. At least for someone new to all of this like me.

"Unca Jon-thn." Close enough. That was so cute. She tried so hard to say that mouthful of words. I hug her close too and breathe in her baby scent.

"I can't believe you're a mom Karlie. She's just perfect." I put my arm around her and we walk towards the front door. Aiden grabbed all of my bags from the trunk and follows us inside.

"How have you been brother? So good to have you home."

"I've been good. Not as good as you though." I smile and motion towards Aiden and Aleah.

"I'm so happy it's almost pathetic!" I see her smile and my heart jumps again. My baby sister has it all. She has always wanted this too so I'm very happy for her.

I can't help but feel a little pang of jealousy though because she

20

SOLDIER'S NEXT JOURNEY

has that perfect life. The life that I've never let myself think I wanted. Until I met Arianna. And Lizzie. Oh my this is going to be tough.

"Your brother has something to tell you. Don't you Jonathan?" Mom says and gives me that look that has always told us she was disappointed in us.

"Yes. Why don't you let me get unpacked and I'll be right back in."

"Okay, I'll be right here. Aleah come sit on Mama's lap. We'll read your book while Uncle Jonathan goes and unpacks."

Mom gives me that stern look again but softens when I give her another hug. She knows I didn't do this on purpose and that I'm going to do what's right. When I figure out what that is.

***

"Miss Arianna would you like some pizza to go with that bacon?" I ask her while playing in her toy kitchen. Marianna bought her this kitchen right after she was born so that she could learn her way around one at an early age. I guess that was her way of doing some of the life lesson teaching.

"Corn!"

"Why thank you I would love some corn on the cob. How did you know?" We laugh as I pretend to eat the plastic piece of corn. That little girl giggle makes my heart leap into my throat when I think of not hearing it every day. If Jonathan wants to take her to Oklahoma I don't know what I'll do.

You can't think like that Lizzie. Stop it.

"Okay Missy let's get you ready for a bath and bed. Go take your clothes off and put them in the hamper. I'll get your water started."

I'm sitting on the floor waiting for the water to warm up when I feel little arms come snaking around my neck.

"Well hello there beautiful. You ready for your bath?" I kiss her cheek and sit her on my lap. I love this little girl so much it's crazy.

"Mama?"

"Mama's in Heaven remember? She's watching you from above the clouds." I lift her into the warm water where she starts to splash around. I smile at her and feel thankful that her attention span is so short. I'm not sure I could handle a lengthy conversation about Marianna.

"Don't splash that much you're getting it all over the floor."

"Spash! Spash!"

"Arianna Elizabeth I said don't splash that much!" That little stinker. She's got such an ornery streak! I haven't a clue where that comes from. Marianna and I were always so straight laced. Jonathan. Must have gotten it from him. I picture a little boy the size of Arianna running around playing cowboys and Indians in the backyard. That little boy looks strangely just like Arianna though.

Please don't let him take her away Marianna. I don't know what I would do without her now. She's all I have left of you.

"Why sad?" I feel a wet little hand touch my cheek and look to see sad little eyes looking into mine.

"I'm not sad sweetheart I was just thinking hard. Are you ready to get washed up?" She nods her head and I busy myself with getting her washed up and ready for bed to keep those devastating thoughts at bay.

"I love you sweet girl. See you in the morning." I kiss her sweet cheek and tuck her in. Before I leave the room I look in one more time to see that she's not holding onto Blankie anymore. She's got Jonathan's teddy bear hugged tight. That's the first time she's ever slept without Blankie. Oh boy this girl might be smarter than we adults are.

I close her door and lean against it needing a second to get ahold of myself. This is all moving so quickly and it scares the tar out of me.

Surely Jonathan has made it home and had time to tell his family. I can't help but wonder how they took the news and if they're on a plane back here to get Arianna. No! Don't think like that Lizzie, that's the worst you can do.

5

"Alright big brother it's time to spill the beans. What has mom so antsy tonight?" Karlie says when I enter the living room again after pacing for ten minutes in my old bedroom.

"Mom? You wanna do the honors?" I smile and squeeze her shoulder knowing full well she's going to make me do this myself.

"Not a chance young man." And she takes a seat in her recliner. That makes me think of when I was a little boy and would get into trouble and she'd make me tell my dad what I had done when he came home.

"Well, long story short. I'll let you start by reading a letter that I got earlier this week when we returned from Iraq."

"You were at Fort Bragg right?"

"Yep. Read it then we'll talk." She looks at mom and all she does is nod her head to her. Thank goodness Karlie took that as enough encouragement and started to read the letter.

I can hear her gasp in all the right places. The same places myself, Tarley and mom had all done.

"Oh my goodness Jonathan! This is incredible but so sad. Can Aiden read it too?"

"Figured he would." I smile a shaky smile and pull up a barstool. This is going to take a while.

"Wow. I don't know what to say man. That's tragic and courageous all in one." Aiden says once he's finished reading the letter too.

"Yes. I feel terrible for Marianna and how she had to have felt in those years she was sick and the last days of her life."

"And to think she still put her daughter first even as she was dying. What an amazing woman she had to have been. Do you remember her at all?" Leave it to Karlie to ask the tough question.

"Kind of. I was in a very bad place after I left here that night. Once I figured out there was going to be that layover I found the nearest bar and tried to drown my sorrows about missing dad's funeral."

"That's completely understandable. No one would blame you for that." Aiden says and everyone else mumbles their agreement.

"Still doesn't make me feel any better knowing I had a child and didn't know. She's almost two years old and I just met her yesterday."

"You did meet her? What does she look like?"

"Just like you Karlie. But she has dark hair." I hand her the picture I've been carrying around in my wallet.

"Oh she is beautiful Jonathan! You did good." She jumps up and hugs me again. I can't help but feel the pride filling up inside me when she reacted that way.

"Thank you I think she's gorgeous too."

"She does look just like you when you were little Karlie." Mom finally says something. I was beginning to think she was asleep. Yea right. She's loving every torturous moment of this.

"Awe I have a mini me finally; since that one looks just like her daddy." She gives Aleah another big hug then kisses Aiden before sitting back down on the couch.

"She's the sweetest little thing too. She loves to swing high and go down the big kid slide on your lap." I know I'm smiling the biggest smile ever telling them about my daughter. Holy crap my daughter! Wow.

"You used to love swinging the highest on the swings too. Karlie would always chicken out and you'd keep going and going until the swing set shook."

"Really? That must be where she gets it then. She wasn't happy until she was really high. Luckily she was in the baby swing and couldn't fall out. Lizzie kept a very close eye on her though."

"Lizzie? You met her too? What's she like?" Karlie gets that out of the whole story? Imagine that.

"She's gentle and kind and definitely loves Arianna."

"Is she hot?" Leave it to Aiden to ask that.

I smile and say, "Of course she was. Couldn't have been ugly or anything."

"Then you need to marry her and bring them here to be with us!"

"Karlie not you too! Mom said the same thing while we were going 70 miles an hour on the highway!"

"Well that should tell you something. When do we get to meet these two beauties in your life?" There's the annoying little sister I've always known. Didn't take her long to get there.

"Karlie slow down. I just met them yesterday. I wanted to come home and tell you guys first before I made a decision. This is all so bizarre to me. I would never have guessed I'd have a little girl anytime soon. Especially without the girlfriend or wife to have her with."

"But you do want to have Arianna at least in your life right?"

"Yes Karlie I do. I just don't know what it is that I need to do here. This is all new to me."

"You wanted our opinions before you made a decision?" Mom asks finally inserting herself into the conversation.

"Of course I did. You're the most important people in my life. Your support means the world to me. You know that right?"

"Of course Karlie and I know you love us but we're just as surprised as you were about Arianna."

"And I knew you would be, that's why I didn't want to tell you over the phone. Now that I'm here and you know all about her, what do you honestly think I should do?"

"Well son what are you going to do about the Army? You need to make that decision before anything else. If you're going to reenlist then you'll need someone to keep Arianna but if you're going to get a regular job then you'll be able to be a father. You also need to decide if you're going to move Arianna here or if you're going to relocate to North Carolina."

"Please tell us it's going to be a job and staying here with her. She needs to be here with her family Jonathan. You need to be around too. For mom, me and everyone else. You've been gone way too long and missed so much."

"Thanks for not making me feel guilty about being away for so long. Geez. I should have known that was coming though."

"We don't mean to be Debbie Downers here brother we just want to help you however we can. Maybe we're a little over the top but we're also excited about having Arianna join our family. And she can be BFF's with Aleah."

"Karlie whoa slow down. Her best friend status is the last thing on my mind right now. Heck I have to pull her from the life she's known and away from the only person she's known."

"I'm sorry Jonathan you're so right. I got caught up in the

excitement of our daughters growing up as close as you and I were."

"Karlie please don't cry. I didn't mean to upset you but you're overlooking the main issues here. Arianna just lost her mom and I'm not sure if it's the best thing for her to lose her aunt and her home so soon too."

"Son, maybe you should go down there and stay until she's used to you then make your decision."

"Mom you're a genius! That sounds like the best thing to do. For now anyway. I don't want to live in North Carolina forever but she does need to get used to me before I decide to move her here to Colvin."

"Maybe you'll even get close to her aunt and she'll come home with you and you'll live happily ever after like me and Aiden!" Karlie laughs that girly laugh she's never outgrown.

"You're impossible! But what's new? Thanks for being so supportive all of you. I love you all very much. I need to go call Lizzie and talk these things over with her. See you later sis. Bye sweet baby girl. So glad I got to meet you finally. Later Aiden."

I walk to my bedroom and shut the door. After talking to my family I feel that me going back there is the best thing for everyone right now. Especially Arianna.

I dial Lizzie's number and wait for her to pick up. Before she does I panic that maybe she's going to ignore my calls and never let me see Arianna again. She wouldn't do that would she?

"Hello Jonathan." Whew she answered. But she sounds asleep and sexy oh my goodness that scratchy voice.

"I'm sorry did I wake you? How far ahead of me are you?"

"No it's fine I just fell asleep reading after I put Arianna to bed.

How was your trip?"

"It was fine. I talked to my mom, sister and brother in law tonight."

"Oh? How did that go? Are you missing any limbs?" She laughs. That sound makes my stomach do flips. What is it about this woman that can make me think about forevers when I talk to her?

"Nah I'm good. They're excited to meet Arianna. And you."

"Meet? Are you taking her away from me already?" She panics and I can clearly hear it in her voice.

"Calm down. I'm not taking her away from you. At least not yet. That's what I wanted to talk to you about. After talking things through with my family we all agree that it might be best for everyone if I come to Temple and stay for a while. So that she can get used to me and vice versa."

"You scared me. I thought you were going to come and yank her away. You coming here and letting yourselves get to know each other is a smart idea. I like it."

"Where do you think I should stay? Is there a hotel there that takes weekly renters?"

"I'll check around for you. How soon do you think you'll be back?" She sounds almost hopeful.

"I'm thinking a couple of days. I need to catch up with a few people here and spend a little time with my family since I've been gone for so long."

"That sounds reasonable. I'll get on the search for your place to stay tomorrow. Are you coming alone?"

"Alone?" She can't mean a girlfriend can she? Didn't I tell her I was single?

"Are any of your family members coming with you?"

"Oh! No they're not coming. No one is ready for that yet."

"Especially not me. I'm sorry that was out of line."

"It's okay Lizzie I know this is tough on you the most."

"I have the most to lose."

"No decisions will be made until we can discuss them and make them together okay?"

"Perfect. Ok well I need to get up and ready for bed so I'll talk to you when you get back. Let me know if you need a ride from the airport."

I can't help but visualize Lizzie getting ready for bed. Snap out of it man you're not helping things!

"I will. Good night Lizzie. Talk to you soon. Just email me the information you find. Thanks for your help."

"Bye Jonathan." And she disconnects the call. I breathe in deep and let it out slowly. This is going to be harder than I ever thought possible. That girl gets my blood pumping just talking to her over the phone, how am I going to see her and be around her every day? Whoa.

***

So he's moving here for a little while. Hmph. Where do I even start to find him somewhere to live? Then it hits me. I should ask the landlord of my apartment building if there's anywhere open for a short term lease. He'd be close and whenever Arianna was with him she'd be close too. Hmmmm.

"Hi Mr. Morgan, it's Lizzie Kentis from 23B. I was wondering if you had anything available for a short term lease? My niece's father is coming to town for a little while and he's needing somewhere to stay while he's here bonding with her. No I don't want him staying with us. I know there's the extra room but we don't know each other that well. I was hoping for somewhere nearby but also not in the same apartment. Okay thank you. Let me know in the next couple of days if you do. Take care thank you."

He doesn't know of anything off hand but he'll call me back. And let him live with us? Is he nuts?? That would never work! Yes she would always be close by but good grief I don't know him well enough to share an apartment with him! That's insane.

At just that moment I visualize Jonathan getting out of the shower and walking around in nothing but a towel wrapped around his waist. Oh no no no not going to happen! Lizzie get your head on your shoulders and out of the gutter! You're an adult, start acting like it!

6

As I get out of the car in front of the 6AB main house I spot AJ walking towards the front yard. He stops to see who has pulled up at his house and then waves when he sees it's me.

"Well if it isn't the soldier returning home from Iraq. Welcome back Jonathan. Good to see you home safely." AJ says and slaps me on the back as he does.

"Good to see you and thank you. How are things going around the 6AB? Doesn't look like much has changed while I've been gone."

"Oh you know same ol' same ol'. How long are you back for this time?"

"I'm not real sure but I'm most likely not reenlisting."

"You've more than served your time son. We're all very proud of you and grateful."

"Thank you sir. I came by to see if Aaron was around? My sister said he might be around here today."

"You're in luck, he's out by the barn. He's replacing one of the stall doors. You know the way. Again, welcome home." He slaps me on the back once more before walking towards the house.

I jog the distance to the barn and find exactly who I was looking for inside. "Hey Aaron what's up?"

"Well if it isn't the soldier boy. How ya been?" Another slap on the back. My back's going to be sore once I've finally seen everyone in town.

"I'm good and you? My sister tells me you've gotten hitched recently?"

"She is correct. I moved back here, met Amie, got married, started another construction company and settled down in Colvin."

"Wow I didn't think you'd ever return."

"I know, it was a messed up deal. I'm sure Karlie would fill you in if you asked."

"Got it. Well, the reason I stopped by was to ask you if you'd have any room on your crew for another? I've been trying to figure out what to do with myself if I don't reenlist."

"Of course. I could always use the help. You here for good now?"

"No, I'm going to North Carolina for a bit and when I come back it'll be for good."

"Well, give me a holler when you're ready for that job. With the list of work I have I'll never run out of things to do."

"I appreciate that. Also, do you know of anywhere I could rent then too?"

"I'll keep my eyes and ears open for ya. Amie and I are building our house right now and we're about ready to move in. Maybe my parents would let you crash in the apartment above the garage?"

"I'll have to talk to them when I get back. Thanks again."

"Later."

All of the Blake men are so accommodating. I'm so happy that my sister married into that family. They're the best one around.

***

"Hi Mr. Morgan yes I was expecting your call. No big deal I was just folding clothes. Oh you do? That would be great. He'll be here in a few days and he's not sure how long he'll be here. A month yes most likely. I'm sure he'd be glad to help fix it up while he's living there. Sure, I'll have him give you a call. His name is Jonathan Doone. Yes sir. He's fresh out of the Army and needing to get his life started. Thank you again Mr. Morgan."

I email the details to Jonathan as soon as I hang up with Mr. Morgan and it's not two minutes before I get a reply back.

Thanks Lizzie. I'll set it up. You're the best. Be there tmrw.

Tomorrow?!?! He's moving here tomorrow? Oh boy.

"Hey pretty girl whatcha doin' in here? You better not have those markers again." I step into Arianna's bedroom and am shocked to find her sitting on her bed snuggling with that darn pink teddy bear.

"Dada dada." Oh brother.

"Is that your teddy bear's name?" Please say yes.

"Dada leave."

"Who's dada?"

"Give Beary."

"Dada gave you the bear?"

"Swide."

"Jonathan you mean?"

"Jon-thin?"

"Yes, the man that went on the slide with you and gave you this bear. His name is Jonathan."

"No dada?"

34

"Um, why don't we color some pictures for a while. Would you like that?" I have got to change this subject before I say the wrong thing.

"When Jon-thin be back?"

"I think he'll come see us tomorrow. I mean come see you tomorrow."

"Yay! See Jon-thin morrow Beary." She seems so happy to see Jonathan. Can't say that I blame her, I kinda feel the same way. Knock it off Lizzie you're setting yourself up for a broken heart.

***

"Well sis, thanks for the ride. Next time I promise I'll have my own vehicle. I think I'll buy a pickup when I get to Charlotte. That way I can take Arianna places without having to burden Lizzie."

"Uh huh I'm sure you'd really be burdening her."

"Karlie. Stop."

"I know, I know. Sorry I can't help myself. Have a good flight big brother. Bring that pretty little girl back with you."

"I will once she's ready."

"And the aunt too. Sorry I'm going! Love you." And she hugs me before escaping out into the crowd entering the airport.

My mother and sister would have Lizzie and I married in a heartbeat if I ever brought her back here. Scary part is I'm not sure that's a bad thing. Doubt she would agree though.

7

Once my flight landed in Charlotte I made my way to baggage claim and towards the taxis. I was just starting to raise my hand for one when I hear a woman saying my name and of course I look around until I see that gorgeous face smiling at me.

"Hey Lizzie what are you doing here? I didn't mean for you to pick me up."

"It's no big deal. I thought it would be nice of us to pick you up. Especially since you don't have wheels of your own."

"Actually I was thinking I need to remedy that problem. Would you be willing to drop me off at a dealership near here?"

"Of course. You're going to just go buy a car?"

"Probably a pickup but yes. I'm going to need a way to get around on my own while I'm here."

"Duh, that does make sense. Which brand of pickup are you wanting?"

"Chevrolet please. I've had my eye on one of the brand new models since they came out."

"They're nice for sure."

"You wanna help me find the right one? Or do you have somewhere to be?"

"No, I don't have anywhere to be. I can help if you think I'd be any."

"You girls are probably going to spend just as much time in it as I will so it makes sense that you'd help."

"Well let's go then. Chevy dealership here we come." She smiles and we drive away from the airport listening to Arianna babble in the backseat. I haven't a clue what she's saying but it sure is animated.

"She's talking a lot more than when I was here last."

"She never stops."

"Uh oh. You must have gotten that from your Aunt Karlie. She never stops either!" I see Lizzie cringe at the mention of Arianna getting something from someone other than herself or Marianna.

"What did your family say about Arianna?"

"They can't wait to meet her. She's family and they love their family."

"It's very weird to think that Arianna has this huge family she's never met when all she has here is me."

"You're part of the family too ya know." She seems surprised to hear me say that.

"Why would I be? I'm just the sister of the dead girl you knocked up."

"Whoa that was harsh Lizzie. Is that really how you feel?"

"I'm so sorry; no that's not how I feel. I'm very worried that that's how you and your family are going to feel."

"Never. You have been there for Arianna for the past two years and you have a strong bond with her. I owe you so much for being there and helping raise her."

"Thank you. Like I've told you before I love her like she were my own."

"I know you do. My family knows that too."

"Ok can we change the subject now? We're almost to the dealership anyway. It's right over there."

"Sure. What color do you think we should choose?"

"We? I think you need to choose the color Jonathan, it's your pickup."

"Right." Wow she's on a roll today. I'm thinking that me being back has made her a lot more nervous than before. "Let's go look at those ones over there. I'm loving the blue."

***

"I can't believe you just bought a new pickup Jonathan."

"Hey I needed one and I've never been able to do that before so I had to do it once to at least say that I have. Right?"

"I guess so. Still think you're crazy." I open the main office door to the apartment complex and introduce Jonathan to Mr. Morgan.

"Mr. Morgan this is Jonathan Doone. He's back and ready for that apartment. I'll go and leave you two to do your business. We're having dinner in about an hour if you're interested in a home cooked meal Jonathan."

"I would love that thanks. I'll see you in an hour." He smiles and I leave the confined space of that small office to make my way to the apartment that I've got to let Jonathan into for the first time.

I hope it's clean enough. I hope it's not too small where he thinks Arianna isn't taken care of enough. What if the food isn't very good and he thinks I'm going to starve her? What if he finds her room too messy or the bathroom not clean?

Breathe Lizzie you're being ridiculous again. You're a good person and your house is a wonderful home for Arianna. Stop freaking out and get your butt up there.

"Thank you for watching her." I had my neighbor watch Arianna while I did the introduction downstairs.

"Lizzie it was only for a few minutes it was no big deal."

"Well I hope you know I appreciated it."

"Of course I do. Now have a good evening dear. That handsome man coming to dinner?"

"Jonathan. Yes. He's Arianna's father so he's here to get to know here and she him."

"How wonderful. So glad he's able to be here now. Your sister really struggled with whether or not to tell him."

"You even knew about him? Good grief who didn't she tell except me?"

"Don't get upset she knew you had enough to deal with. She was so grateful to you."

"I know. It just feels like when it came to Jonathan everyone knew so much more about him than me and I'm the one that needed to know the most!"

"It's frustrating but your sister knew what she was doing. It might not seem like it now but she really did."

"If you say so. Thanks again for watching Arianna. I really have to get dinner started. See you later."

"Goodbye dear. Anytime, I'm just next door." She gives me a tender hug and leaves my apartment. Now, I must get dinner started and it has to be fantastic! But what would I be able to make that Jonathan would think was fantastic? His mother probably makes four course meals that make mine look like an appetizer.

Stop it Lizzie. Who cares if he likes your food or not? Arianna loves your cooking and that's all that matters. If he doesn't like it he can makes his own! And I'll tell him that if he complains at all!

8

I stop in the bathroom and look once again at myself in the mirror.
I'm supposed to be up in Lizzie's apartment in a few minutes for
dinner and I'm so nervous I'm beside myself. I've become a
hormonal teenage boy again who can't stop looking at himself in
the mirror before his first date. Good grief get a grip man!

Well here we go. I shut my door and take the stairs to the second
level. Once outside of Lizzie's door I see a woman stick her head
out of her own door and wave. I lift my hand and wave back while
smiling. Feeling a little strange I knock on 23B and wait for the
woman swirling in my brain to open.

I get a shock when it's actually a little woman that answers the
door and wraps herself around my legs. I look up at Lizzie who is
standing a few feet back from us. She has the strangest look on her
face like she can't believe the way Arianna is acting around me.

"Well hello pretty girl. How are you?" I lift Arianna up and give
her a kiss on her forehead. That seems so natural now I almost
don't realize I've done it until I see Lizzie's face change again.
This time to panic. She really is terrified I'm going to take
Arianna away from her.

"Dada dada dada!" Arianna says and kisses my cheek while
wrapping her little arms all the way around my neck.

I can feel myself stiffen with shock at the words she's saying and
immediately look at Lizzie. She is also in a state of shock and
unease.

"I don't know what else to do to distract her from that." She
doesn't move a muscle, just stands there staring.

"It's okay, maybe we should tell her then? She seems to have
picked up on it somehow." I set Arianna down and she takes my
hand while pulling me towards the hallway behind Lizzie.

"Where are we going squirt?" I look at Lizzie questioningly.

"Her bedroom. She must want to show you where her room is. I'll just go finish up dinner and holler for you two when it's ready." And she walks away a little faster than needed.

"Is this your bedroom Arianna?" I say as she pulls me into a pink and purple bedroom. I can't help but feel a little uneasy in a room so girly. I almost feel like an outsider. She doesn't seem to feel the same way though as she pulls me down to sit on her bed.

"Dada sit. Me cook." And she toddles off to the little plastic kitchen on the other side of the room. She comes back with what looks like a hotdog and a corn on the cob.

"Oh that looks good. Thank you." I pretend to eat the food as she watches my every move.

"Dada want eat more?" She asks from in front of me. I look down and she has both of her tiny little hands on my knees. The stark difference in our sizes makes my heart completely fill with so much emotion. This is my little girl and I will forever get to see her get bigger until she no longer wants to play with plastic food.

"Sure I'll eat more." I give the hotdog and corn back to her and she replaces it with a banana. Such a giving little thing.

"Dinner is ready when you two are." Arianna and I are both a little startled when we hear Lizzie say from the doorway. She looks very uncomfortable and upset.

"Lizzie are you okay?" I stand up and walk towards her.

"I'm fine." She turns and walks quickly back to the kitchen and dining room area. She is visibly upset but I don't have a clue what to say or do to make it better.

"Arianna, dinner's ready. Let's go have some real food." I hold out my hand for her to take it and when she does we walk hand in hand to the table.

My heart is so full of love right now it might burst. Not sure I can handle much more.

***

Arianna is having no trouble at all adjusting to Jonathan and his being in our house. The house seems so much smaller now that he's in it. And everything seems so much more real now too.

I walked into Arianna's room expecting to see Jonathan standing and her not really knowing what to say to him. Boy was I wrong. I walk in and find him sitting on her bed and her standing there with her hands on his knees. It looked so innocent and natural.

I'm going to lose her. Not IF any more but WHEN.

"Arianna we need to get you washed up before you get in your high chair." I start to walk to pick her up but she turns to Jonathan first.

"Dada wash me." And he looks up at me with his eyes the size of half dollars clearly as shocked as I am by her continued use of the word.

"Sure let's go to the kitchen sink. I'm sorry Lizzie. I don't know what else to do but just go with it." He shrugs and give me an 'I'm sorry' look.   I shrug and continue serving up Arianna's dinner.

I feel so out of place here that it's almost like I'm intruding on their lives. This is my home but now I feel as though it's not mine anymore but Arianna's and I'm just staying here.

Until Jonathan takes her to her forever home. Oh boy.

"Please don't be upset with me or her." I feel a hand on my shoulder and it makes me weak in the knees. I suck in a quick breath of shock and look up into the most gorgeous eyes I think I've ever seen.

"It's um, um ok. Let's eat." I take a slight step away and turn to Arianna who's waiting to go in her chair. I lift her up and kiss her forehead praying she knows how much I love her.

"Thanks again for getting the apartment arranged for me while I'm here. You went above and beyond for me and I really appreciate it." He smiles that smile at me that makes my stomach do flips.

I sure hope he can't see the reaction my body and heart seems to have to him. This is ridiculous like a teenager with her first crush.

"It was really no problem. I just called Mr. Morgan. He figured the rest out." I can't make eye contact. Don't make eye contact.

"Dada eat?" Arianna pulls me out of the coma I seemed to be in there and of course I can't help but look at Jonathan waiting to see his reaction.

"Can I tell her? It's killing me hearing it and not being able to respond." He pleads with me with a pained look on his face.

"Don't think we have a choice. Obviously she's smarter than we are." I throw up my hands in defeat and sigh.

"Arianna I am your Dada. Do you know that?" Jonathan says and smiles at her.

"You Dada? You Dada! You Dada!" And she slaps her hands on the tray sending food everywhere. Including all over the front of Jonathan's shirt.

"I think that's your Dada initiation." I laugh and get up to get a towel.

"I'm oddly okay with that to be honest. A week ago I would have flipped out if someone got stuff all over my clothes but today it feels normal." He smiles at me and once again I'm at a loss for words. Or breath.

9

"Thank you for dinner Lizzie. It was wonderful." I hug her and immediately wonder what I'm doing. I jerk back when I feel her stiffen.

"Um, you're welcome. Say goodbye Arianna." She points to me in hopes of changing the subject from the hug I just gave her.

"I'm sorry about that. I'm so used to hugging everyone back at home when we leave. Please forgive me."

"It's okay. It just catches me off guard. It's um, well nice." She says wringing her hands in front of her.

She's affected by me too. Hmmm but does that change anything? No. I'm here for Arianna. Only Arianna.

"See you two tomorrow. I'll be working on the apartment most of the night and day tomorrow so whenever you're up and about come on down and maybe we can go get some breakfast?" The things that come out of my mouth anymore are never what I think they'll be.

"Sure. I'm not sure if it'll be for breakfast but at least lunch if not. Have fun." She smiles and opens the front door for me reminding me that I need to walk out of it and walk back to my own temporary apartment.

"See you two later. Good bye Arianna." I kiss her forehead and she kisses my cheek back while waving her chubby little hand.

"Bye bye Dada!" She smiles and it makes the butterflies start to swarm and the warmth to enter my heart a bit more. I love this little girl already, so much it's scary.

"Bye sweetheart. See you tomorrow." I touch the back of her head and wink at Lizzie. If I didn't know better I would think she reddened a little. Surely not. I'm not so sure she even likes me.

Once the door is shut behind me I turn to walk towards my apartment and I hear someone call my name from behind me. Thinking it's Lizzie not wanting me to leave I turn with a huge smile on my face. But it's not Lizzie just the nosey old lady who waved at me earlier.

"How do you know my name?" I ask while walking closer to her.

"Oh I know all about you Soldier Man." And she smiles so big I'm not sure she can any bigger.

"You do? Lizzie tell you about me I take it?" I'm intrigued now.

"Nope. That would be Marianna who told me all about you."

"Really? I didn't think she gave me much thought. Lizzie didn't know about me but you do?" I'm very interested now.

"Oh yes we talked in great lengths about you over the years."

"So you know that I didn't know about Arianna, right?"

"Yes I do. I know you just got her letter. And you're here, so that's a good thing young man."

"Where else would I be? I found out I have a little girl."

"A weak man would have continued on without making that leap of faith."

"I'm not a weak man."

"And that Marianna told me too. She didn't know you very well but she did know that you would do the right thing once you heard about the baby."

"I wish I would have known all along. I've missed so much."

"Yes you have but you also have the rest of your life now to spend with her."

"That is true."

"Are you going to stay here or move her back to Oklahoma?"

"I don't have a clue yet. I'm so torn over that decision."

"But you're going to stay for a bit and get to know the baby?"

"Yes I am."

"And the aunt?"

"Well yes, she's part of it."

"Is she? Marianna had hoped you two could get along well and do the best thing for her daughter. Your daughter."

"I'm honestly trying to do just that. It's just so bizarre. I think I've used that word more in the past week than I ever have in my life."

"That's a good definition."

"Sometimes I feel like I'm in an alternate universe but then I see Arianna's face or she calls me Dada and it hits me that it's all real."

"She's a smart little cookie."

"That she is. I told her tonight that I am her Dad. But of course it affected me and Lizzie more than her."

"Is there a you and Lizzie?"

"Um, no I didn't mean it like that."

"Uh huh. Well young man I better let you get back to working on that apartment. Take care and don't be a stranger."

"Thank you." This woman know everything. She would fit in at home.

"Go slow and be easy. She's scared right now and holding on tighter than she needs to be. She'll finally see that one day."

"Um, okay. Thanks." I'm not sure who she's talking about but okay.

***

"Okay Missy let's get you in the bath and ready for bed." This night has got to end soon. I'm not sure I can handle much else. Having Jonathan here in this apartment was so awkward but comfortable at the same time.

"Dada home?" She asks as I lift her into the water.

"Yes he went to his home. Ready for a bath?" Distraction number one.

"Dada no stay here?" Oh boy.

"No he has his own apartment. We'll go see it tomorrow."

"O-tay. Me go Dada home morrow?"

I can't speak so I simply nod my head. She seems to be okay with that reply and starts to splash in the water.

If only it were that easy for me to forget about tonight and everything else that's going on in my head. And heart. And body. Grrrr!

"Night sweet baby girl. I'll see you in the morning. Sweet

dreams."

"Night night mama." That was strange she never tells Marianna goodnight unless we've just had a conversation about her. Oh well she's had a long day.

We both have. I think I'll take a long hot bath myself before bed. Maybe that way I can relax. Please let me relax.

After filling the tub and adding my bubble bath I climb in and feel the release of tension all over my body the farther in I go. This feels so amazing. This should help just fine.

10

"Lizzie I can't stop thinking about you. I can't stop seeing that beautiful mouth smile that amazing smile at me. I can't stop thinking about how it would feel to touch those lips with my own."

"Jonathan I can't stop either. Please kiss me." And he wraps his arms around me and kisses me like I've never been kissed before.

Sparks and fireworks are going off everywhere. I can't see or breathe. The feeling is so overwhelming that I can't seem to catch my breath. Oh Jonathan what have you done to me? You've taken my breath away completely and I feel as though I'm suffocating from it.

Wait!?!? Suffocating? I jolt upright and realize I had been lying in the bathtub still and as I look around frantic for Jonathan I realize I was having a dream. A very steamy dream. So steamy I had slid down into the water and was trying to breathe under the water. Hence the suffocating. It was actually drowning.

"I seriously just fell asleep in the tub and had a sexy dream about Jonathan! Oh my goodness I really have lost it!" I flip the drain and listen to the water start slipping down the pipe. I cannot believe I just had such a good dream about Jonathan and about drowned. Wait? Good dream? This is going to be a very long night. Ugh!

I lay in bed for a while but know I'm never going to be able to sleep. My head is too jumbled up to get any sleep…

I put my robe on and walk out the back door onto the balcony where I see that my neighbor is also sitting out on hers.

"Couldn't sleep either?"

"No, I couldn't. What's your excuse?" She asks as I sit down in a chair closest to the wall separating our balconies.

"I've got so much on my mind it's ridiculous."

"And he's very good looking too."

"What?! Who?"

"Oh yes, don't act like he's not the reason you're out here tonight unable to get to sleep."

"What are you talking about?"

"Jonathan."

"Oh, well he's not the reason I'm not asleep."

"Who are you trying to convince? Me or you?"

"Whatever. Maybe I'll just go for a little walk around the courtyard. Will you step in and listen for Arianna since you're already out here?"

"Of course. Have a good walk." She winks at me and walks back into her house. I walk to my front door, unlock it and let her in. She's smiling like she's got a guilty secret or something. Crazy old lady. I can't help but smile as I shut the door and start my late night walk. How could she possibly know he's the reason I couldn't sleep? Surely I didn't make any noise while I was dreaming or drowning. Good grief what an idiot.

***

I think that's the last cupboard door. I've taken each of them off, cleaned, sanded and re-stained it. They look so much better now. When I'm done with this place it'll be a great family home. I can't help but envision my own family being in here. Me and Arianna living together and being a family. With Lizzie. That should scare me but it really doesn't. It's almost comforting to think she'll always be around. For Arianna. Only Arianna. Uh huh you keep

52

telling yourself that man.

I shake my head knowing I need to quit thinking like this about a girl I just met. She's got her own life that doesn't involve me and most likely never will past what has to do with Arianna.

"What're you shaking your head for?" I jump and turn around quickly to see Lizzie standing in my front doorway with a smile on her face. An almost mischievous look because she knew she was going to startle me.

"What in the world are you doing here? You scared the living daylights out of me!"

"I kinda figured it would. I was out for a walk and saw your lights were on. I knocked but you didn't hear me so I tried the knob and it was open so I came in."

"Well I'm glad you did but I think you took ten years off my life!"

"Good thing I can take care of Arianna when you expire early."

"You're a pain in the butt aren't you?"

"I've been told that a few times in my life. Anyway, you've done great things so far with this place. I saw it when the last family moved out and it was horrible."

"Thank you. I enjoy using my hands to make something better. Ya know?"

"Military thing?"

"No, growing up with my Dad kind of thing."

"Mr. Fix It?"

"He was. I always tried to help him. But once I enlisted I missed that most. The being able to transform something myself.

Spending that time with my Dad growing up was priceless. I know that now that he's gone."

"I'm sorry you weren't able to be there for the funeral."

"Thank you. I'm over it now but it was very tough. Toughest thing I've ever dealt with. Knowing my sister and mother dealt with it alone. While I was off doing my own thing."

"Your own thing? You were serving your country Jonathan. Nothing selfish about that."

"Maybe, but I still felt terrible for not being around."

"That's understandable but I can guarantee you that your mom and sister are very proud of you for what you've done with your life. Heck I am and I just met you. Your daughter will be too one day when she is old enough to understand."

"Wow you're really on a roll tonight. I needed a cheerleader. Thank you."

"I was a cheerleader throughout middle school and high school. Must come naturally." She laughs and walks closer to me and grabs the paint brush I had sitting on the stain lid.

"You're good at it. You made me feel all mushy inside."

"Mushy? You big and strong soldier? Mushy? Right." She flips the brush towards me not realizing it was covered in stain. Just as she does about twenty globs hit my shirt and face.

"What are you doing woman?" Thankfully I got my eyes closed before that could get in them. I lift the bottom of my T-shirt up and wipe my face and as I do I see Lizzie freeze in place. She looks like she was caught doing something wrong by her parents.

"What's wrong Lizzie? I know you didn't mean to." I reach out and take the brush from her hand. As I sit it down I look back at her and see that she's staring at my chest. Horrified.

"It's okay it's an old shirt. I'll just take it off and get a new one on. No biggie." I quickly slip the shirt over my head and see Lizzie go wide eyed again.

"Lizzie are you okay? Seriously it's okay. I'll just get another shirt."

"Um um um yes I'm fine. I'm so sorry I ruined your shirt."

"It's fine. I'll be right back."

***

Holy crap I about bit my tongue off when I saw Jonathan lift his shirt up. Then he had to go and take it all the way off. Be still my heart. Heck more like hormones. I have got to quit looking at this guy like he's a possibility. He isn't.

"I really am sorry Jonathan. I'll buy you another shirt tomorrow." He comes back with a new shirt on. Darn.

"Don't worry about it. It's an old one. No harm done." He smiles and my insides do flips again. Dang it how can this guy do such wild things to my insides with just a smile? I'm in trouble.

"So, what do you have left to do in the apartment?"

"I'm going to do the backsplash and floor in the kitchen. Then probably lay hardwood throughout the rest of it."

"Oh Jonathan that's going to look great!"

"I think it will. It's going to be a great home for a nice family when I'm done."

"I might hire you to change some of our apartment when you're done!" That sounded dumb. Why did I say that? Why would he want to stay here and get paid to do my place? Dumb dumb dumb.

"I wouldn't charge you but could do some upgrades if you two need it."

"Nah we're all good. Um, I guess I had better head back to the apartment. The neighbor is staying there while I go for my walk."

"She's quite the spit fire isn't she?"

"Oh yes. Likes to butt into places she doesn't belong."

"Yes she does and seems to have the inside scoop about everything." Big smile. Oh gosh what does that mean? Did she says something to him about me? She better not have! I'll have to interrogate her when I get back.....

"Do you want a beer?"

"I would actually. Thank you." Maybe that will help me relax and not be so nervous around him.

He walks to the fridge and I can't help but look at his backside. Beautiful backside actually. I feel another blush creeping up my neck. Stop it Lizzie!

"Are you feeling okay? You look flushed." He smiles knowing full well he's making me nervous.

"I'm fine thanks. Nothing this cold beer won't help."

"While you're here I could use a woman's opinion on the paint color for in here. Do you think yellow, tan or blue?"

"Oh I love that blue color. It's such a soft shade but gives you more than just white. That will look great."

"That's what I was thinking too. I may use it throughout the kitchen, dining room and living room."

"That sounds right. I can't wait to see it done. If you need help painting just let me know. I'd love to help." And spend more time with you wouldn't hurt.

"I may take you up on that. I could use your help with the bathroom tonight if you're game. I'm just painting it a light gray color."

"Sure, I can get these clothes dirty. Give me a brush and I'll get started."

"Really? You don't mind helping this late?"

"I'm an artist, there is no bad time to paint."

"Good point. Here you can use this brush." His hands grip over mine after I take it from his hands. He hangs on for a bit longer than needed and looks straight into my eyes. Oh boy what have I gotten myself into tonight?

"Thanks I'll be done in a bit." I smile and might have swayed my hips a little more than needed on the short walk to the bathroom. I turn just before entering the room and see that Jonathan has definitely been watching the show I put on. I smile and see him take a deep breath and walk back to the kitchen. One point for Lizzie. I can't help but smile at that.

***

That girl is going to kill me. After watching her walk to the bathroom swaying like she's dancing, I could use a cold shower. But she's in the only bathroom. Wonderful.

Then of course my mind starts to conjure up thoughts of what could happen if I were to go into said bathroom with said beautiful woman with said shower. Oh boy. I shake my head to get those sexy thoughts out of it. I can't do that! She's off limits you idiot.

After what seemed like forever I heard Lizzie call out for me.

"Jonathan, can you come help me reach please?"

I could help you reach all right. STOP IT! Good grief man get a grip.

"Sure what do you need to reach?" I say as I turn into the doorway of the bathroom. I stop dead in my tracks because Lizzie has taken off her shirt and is standing there in a sports bra and short shorts. Holy smokes I about swallow my tongue.

She must have noticed me staring and she says, "It got hot in here."

"Hey no problem. Where do you need to reach?" Head shake number fifty.

"I need to reach up there above the shower. I can't get the stool in there and reach at the same time."

"I'll get it. Hand me the brush." I take the brush from her and feel the electric spark again when our hands touch. I turn and step onto the side of the bathtub and reach up to touch the unpainted spot.

"All better. You're already done in here? It looks great thank you." I step down from the side of the tub and realize that Lizzie is standing directly in front of me with her back to the wall. I reach back and feel that I'm butted up against the vanity too leaving only an inch between us.

I look down into her face and see her eyes saying the same thing I'm thinking. I reach my hand up and touch her lips. They open slightly as she sucks in a quick breath.

That's all it took and she leaps into my arms which go around her as quickly as I can. She molds herself to me and I can't help but moan as she presses her lips to mine. Talk about fireworks! This woman makes me light up in ways I've never known were possible.

She also moans into my mouth as she opens hers and I slip my tongue inside. I lean forward which makes Lizzie tightly fitted between myself and the wall. She feels so amazing against my hard body and I know I had to have moaned again because of the feelings rushing through me.

I run my hands all over her bare skin that isn't covered by the sports bra. She has the softest skin I've ever felt. She smells like Heaven and I can't seem to stop myself as I deepen the kiss even more.

I feel her hands roaming over my shoulders and head as she pulls my hair. That pulls me even closer and other parts of me come even more alive.

"Lizzie you're so beautiful. What are you doing to me?" I say lightly as I kiss down her neck. But as I do I realize I shouldn't have said anything because she freezes and lets go of my hair.

"I can't do this. It's so wrong. I'm so sorry Jonathan." She pushes me away and runs to the front door and leaves the apartment in haste.

Dang it! Why the heck did I say anything to her? I ruined the moment. But she would have regretted it forever if I hadn't. Would I have regretted it too?

11

"Well hello Missy where have you been?"

"I went for a walk. Why?" I ask my neighbor when I walk into the safety of my apartment. A place that's safe from the pull Jonathan has on me.

"Why are you all flushed and nervous?"

"I ran the rest of the way back so I'm a little hot."

"Just from the run or did you see that handsome soldier man?" She winks at me. Winks, really?

"Running. Jonathan has nothing to do with it. You can go now thanks." That might have been a little rude but I open the front door hoping she'll get the hint. I really don't want to talk about what sent me running home. Especially not with her since she seems to be Jonathan's #1 fan.

"Well, let me know if you need anything else. Or to talk. I've got a great listening ear. Your sister used to use it a lot." She touches my shoulder lightly and smiles before heading out the door.

"Thank you but I'm good." I can't talk about this attraction with Jonathan. It'll be real then and I can't have it be real. Arianna would be the one to get the raw end of that. Can't can't can't.

I open Arianna's door to peek in on her and start to feel more at peace when I see her sweet little face. Watching her sleep has been something I've enjoyed doing since she was a baby. She always looks so peaceful when asleep and I know that's how I always want her to feel even when she's awake.

Which is another reason I can't let anything happen between Jonathan and myself. It will only end horribly and have more impact on Arianna than it will on us. She doesn't deserve any more hurt than she's had already in her short little life. Losing her mom was I hope the most painful thing she ever has to endure. If only I could protect her for the rest of her life.

I sit down next to her on her tiny bed and run my hand along her soft cheek. My heart grows so much when I look at this sweet little girl and I believe it always will. She's like my little girl instead of my little niece.

Maybe most of my anxiety towards Jonathan is that I'm jealous that he is her biological father and I'm just her mom's sister. Marianna left Arianna with me knowing I would love her as my own and I do more than I ever thought possible. I just can't help but be drawn to Arianna's dad too.

Ok sis, did you know I was going to be attracted to him like this? Was this your master plan? Well, if it was it's working. But I can't do this to Arianna sis. Help me figure this out please. This is all your fault ya know!

I can't help but feel guilty after saying that last part because I know my sister would have much rather been here to take care of her own child. But she did open the can of worms where Jonathan is concerned. Ugh this is so confusing and I'm exhausted already and he just got here. Wonderful.

***

After Lizzie left last night I had a hard time sleeping so this morning I need to get some strong coffee before going up to see Arianna. If it would only hurry up and finish brewing. I need to get up there before I lose my nerve.

Once I have a cup in my belly and a refill in my hands, I step out my door and see Lizzie's neighbor standing against the front of my new pickup.

"Hello young man. Long night?" She smiles.

"Um yes I was working on the kitchen most of it. What can I help you with?"

"I was wondering what your intentions are with Arianna and Lizzie."

"Intentions? What do you mean?" I'm thoroughly confused now. What is this crazy old lady talking about now?

"Are you going to take little Arianna away from Lizzie or are you going to marry Lizzie and make them a real family?"

I about choke on the coffee I was taking a sip of.

"You're bold and don't beat around the bush do you?"

"Who needs bushes? Answer the question young man."

"Wow. I'm only taking it day by day with Arianna. She needs to get used to me being her dad and being around before I make any decisions about her future."

"That's fair. But what about Lizzie?"

"What about her? I'm not obligated to her in any way."

"Maybe not but I see a good thing there and I would hope you're smart enough to see it too. Have a good day soldier man." And she walks the opposite way of her apartment.

Wow she's something alright. I wonder if she's had this conversation with Lizzie too? Goodness I hope not. She'll be completely skittish today if that's the case. Our encounter last night is going to be hard enough for her to deal with today. I feel bad but it was so amazing that I'm having a hard time feeing too terrible about it.

"What are you smiling about?" I hear from above me on the stairs and I about fall backwards out of fear. Lizzie. What is it with this woman and sneaking up on me and scaring the daylights out of me?

"You're too sneaky for your own good. One of these days you're going to make me have a heart attack." I smile up at her feeling relieved she isn't acting strange.

"Sorry we were going down and saw you coming up. When I saw you weren't paying attention to where you were going I might have seen an opportunity to get the upper hand." And she smiles that life altering smile which makes me about fall backwards down the stairs.

"Such a pest. Hi sweet girl how are you this morning?" I lean down and pick up Arianna. Kissing her on the forehead seems so natural now and automatic I guess. My heart feels like it grew even bigger when she leaned up and gave me a big sloppy kiss on the cheek.

"Dada dada dada." She lays her head on my shoulder and my world tilted a bit. I lift my eyes and look at Lizzie and smile. She's actually smiling at us this time instead of looking like she's seeing the worst thing she could see.

"She missed you this morning. She couldn't wait any longer so we're coming to see if you're ready for some breakfast."

"Well I missed her too. I wasn't sure if I would see you today after last night." I see her look down at her feet with the mention of that.

"It can't happen again. I should have never let it happen in the first place. I'm sorry. Can we forget it ever happened?" She finally looks up at me and I can clearly see the confusion in her eyes. Good she's as mixed up as I am right now. I can't help but smile at that thought.

"We can start over but I can't forget it." She frowns and I can see her tightening her fists at her side and relaxing them. I think she's nervous.

"Well I guess that's better than nothing. What are you smiling about?"

"Oh nothing. Where do you want to go for breakfast Arianna?" We need a change of subject before Lizzie runs away like a scared little girl.

"Her favorite place is the pancake place over on Gordon Road. Want me to drive?"

"Sure. I need to go get a car seat today while we're out. You can help me pick it out since I'm sure you know more than I do about what I need to get."

"You'll get there don't worry." She could see the regret on my face. I should know what seat is needed for my own little girl but like she said I'll get there. Someday I hope. Someday soon.

"Thanks. I can't help but feel like I'm behind and trying to catch up to the rest of the group."

"Marianna and I had to learn just like you are. Don't sweat it, really. It's not that big of a deal. You're here and that's the biggest thing."

"I wouldn't be anywhere else." I put Arianna in her seat and once I get her buckled in I kiss her forehead again. It's amazing how quickly my heart was consumed by this little human.

"Dada wuv you." She smiles that slobbery grin and I fell even farther in love with my little angel.

"She turns the big ol' soldier into mush!" I hear Lizzie laugh as I get in the passenger side of her car. Looking up at her I see she's smiling just as big as Arianna was. Damn, this woman is driving me insane!

"Shush."

"Nothing to be embarrassed by. All good daddy's love their babies."

"I'm not embarrassed in the least. I do love her though. I understand why you're so attached to her."

She frowns and starts the engine clearly ending this conversation. She's still afraid I'm going to take Arianna away from her. Hmmmm what am I supposed to be doing here?

***

What am I going to do when Jonathan is ready to go back to Oklahoma? I know he's going to take Arianna with him. How do I live without her though? But I can't expect him to leave her here with me either. Ugh!

The rest of the way to the restaurant I know I'm in a terrible mood now and not very talkative. Jonathan knows why I'm upset and goes easy on me instead of pushing me to converse with he and Arianna.

They're carrying on quite a conversation and I feel like a cab driver or something that doesn't exist in their world, only driving them where they need to go. I've never felt so uncomfortable around Jonathan as I do now. This is all so awkward and last night's situation didn't help AT ALL!

"We're here Arianna. Ready for some pancakes?" I put the car in park and turn off the engine. Before I can get my seatbelt off Jonathan jumps out and runs around to my side of the car opening my door for me.

"Chivalry isn't dead. Thank you." But before I can turn around to shut my door he turns me around and puts his hands on my shoulders.

"Lizzie I know none of this is easy for either one of us. I want you to know that I'm not just going to cut you out of her life. You believe me don't you?"

"Yes but I can't help but be afraid of losing her though."

"I know. This isn't an ideal situation but we'll figure it out."

"Ok. Let's get some breakfast. Arianna and I are starved."

"Good idea. I'll get the little angel. You get her bag."

"Deal." That seemed so natural. Almost too comfortable. Most parents do this type of thing but I can't let myself get too comfortable with it. Jonathan and I aren't her parents. He is.

"Stop thinking about it all. Just breathe Lizzie." He bumps my hip with his while we walk to the front door of the restaurant. I look up at him and take a deep breath. Oh boy I shouldn't have done that. There's not enough oxygen in the world to help ease the feeling he gives me.

12

"What is such a beautiful family up to today?" Lizzie and I freeze and glance at each other quickly when we hear the waitress say while I'm handing her the money.

"Um, we're going to the zoo." I say not sure what to really say in this situation. I don't want to embarrass Lizzie but for some reason I liked the waitress calling us a family. Man you have got to get a grip.

"We're not a family, well we are but not that kind." Lizzie says before she turns and quickly exits the restaurant.

"I'm sorry I didn't mean to intrude. I just assumed you were married with a little girl. Very sorry." An embarrassed red tint covers the poor girl's face.

I smile and simply say, "It's not a big deal. Have a good day."

Why did it freak Lizzie out so much to be associated as a family with me and Arianna? Could she be embarrassed to be thought of as my wife? Am I that repulsive? Hmm.

"Well you sure hightailed it out of there like you were on fire. What gives?" I say to her once I'm in the car.

Lizzie keeps herself busy starting the car and backing out of our spot trying not to make eye contact with me. Once she's put her foot on the brake to shift into gear, I put my hand on hers.

"Lizzie, what gives? Are you okay?"

"I'm fine. I need to drive though we're blocking traffic."

I look around and see no traffic. What is up with this crazy woman? Just when I think I'm making progress understanding her she throws me another curve ball. Ugh.

***

That woman thinking Jonathan and I were married made me feel so good so quickly that it scared me. It's too easy for me to be with him and Arianna. Too easy to put myself into the wife/mother role and it's going to do nothing but hurt me.

"Where to now?" I ask him hoping he says his house.

"I'd like to go get a few things for Arianna for my place if that's okay."

"Sure. You wanna go to the mall or what?"

"You tell me. I've never been here before."

"We'll have to go into Charlotte if you want to go to the big mall."

"Nah I'm good with the little one here. Maybe we can take Arianna to see that new kid's movie too while we're here." He smiles at me and the butterflies take light again.

"Sure. I don't have anything else to do today. Wanna see the movie Arianna?" She smiles and squeals with happiness.

"I'd take that a yes. Dadda's gonna get you some things for his house too."

"Toys. Toys. Toys."

"Yes some toys too." He smiles again and shakes his head. I should just drop these two off and go home to my own house. I'm not sure I can deal with him gradually taking Arianna and her love away from me.

"I think I should just let you two spend this time together and see you both when you get back to the apartment."

"Lizzie, calm down. What is up with you? We want you to spend the day with us. Why wouldn't we?" He touches my cheek with his hand and I about jump out the window and see him staring at me like I have two heads.

"Um I just wasn't sure if this needed to be a daddy/daughter day or not. I don't mind leaving you two alone." I try to open my door but Jonathan leans over and takes my hand off the door handle.

Oh my goodness he is so close and I'm afraid to turn my head around so I continue to look out my window. If I don't turn around I won't find him in kissing distance again. The butterflies are multiplying like rabbits.

"Lizzie look at me." I hear his voice next to my right ear.

"I slowly turn my head but lean back towards the door as far as I can. There's no way I can handle being face to face with him in these close quarters.

"What are you scared of? You're acting like a whipped pup. What the heck is going on with you?"

"I'm just tired. Didn't sleep much last night. I'm sorry."

"I'm sorry you're suffering so much. I don't mean for you to be hurting."

"I know. Can we just go in?" I start to open the car door again and hear him sigh.

"Lizzie I'm not going to just rip her away from you. You don't need to worry about that."

This time it's my turn to sigh. "I know you say that Jonathan but you can't live here forever. Eventually you're going to want to get back to Oklahoma and to your life."

"Eventually yes but not right this second. And not until we have both come to an agreement about what to do."

"TOYS!!!!!" Thank goodness Arianna chose that moment to have a breakdown. We both turn to look at her.

"Ok angel, let's go get you some new toys." Jonathan opens his car door and then Arianna's.

While he's lifting her out of her car seat I see she is laying her head on his shoulder. She already loves him like any daughter would. I'm seriously fighting a losing battle here. Jonathan may say he'll never take her away from me, but I know deep down it'll happen and way before I'm ready for it to.

13

Spending this day with Arianna and Lizzie has been great. I've gotten a bunch of toys and even a bed for my house. Arianna picked out mermaid bedding and a closet full of new clothes too. I'd say she's set to have more than just a few hours at my place.

But how do I start this conversation with Lizzie without her losing her mind again like earlier?

As we gather all of the shopping bags and start towards my apartment I decide to take the opportunity to talk to Lizzie.

"So, would you be okay with me keeping Arianna here with me tonight? At least see if she'll do it?" I look at Lizzie but see she's closing her eyes and taking deep breaths.

"Yes I suppose it's the next step now that you have a house that's going to be equipped for a little girl." She won't look at me. I know this is breaking her heart but she has to realize that I want to spend time with my little girl just like she does.

"So you'll be okay with it?"

"Yes. We can sure see if she'll make it through the night." I'll go get her favorite pajamas and her teddy bear." Just like that Lizzie heads out the door and towards her own apartment.

"Well angel do you want to spend the night with Dada in your new room?" That is hoping the delivery guys bring her bed and dresser soon.

As if they heard me, a knock sounds on the door. I open it to find two grimy looking guys on the other side holding the twin size mattress I had just purchased.

"Where do we take this man?" The tallest of the men asks me.

"In the first room on the right. Thank you." I look around outside hoping Lizzie doesn't come back until these unpleasant men are gone.

Hmm I'm protective of her already? I've got to get a grip.

After the guys get all the parts to the room brought in I say, "Thanks guys I can take it from here."

I usher them towards the door and Lizzie picks that exact moment to walk through the front door. I see the second she realizes the men are standing there with me and looking at her like she's a piece of meat.

I clear my throat and open the front door trying to make it clear that they needed to leave and stop ogling Lizzie.

"Well aren't you a sexy piece of Heaven. Quite the sight for sore eyes today sweetheart." The shorter guy hisses out and whistles.

The instant Lizzie hears what he says she turns around and smacks him right across the face.

All three of us men step back in shock. She seriously just smacked him!

"Didn't your mother ever tell you not to talk to women like that?"

"Well, I take it back. We're outta here. You're not near as sweet as you look. Good day sir." And they're gone.

I turn around and look at Lizzie not sure what to say. I think I just fell a little bit more in love with this woman and I'm not sure what to do about it.

"Don't look at me like that. He had it coming. I'm sorry you had to see it though. Thank goodness Arianna wasn't here to see it."

"I am so glad I was here to see that. That was the single most amazing thing I've ever seen!" I walk to her and hug her but she's stiff as a board at first. Then she relaxes in my arms and actually puts her arms around my waist.

"Um, I think this is all you need for her first overnight." Lizzie finally says and steps back out of my arms once again not wanting to look me in the eyes.

"I'm sorry about that. I just can't believe you just did that! Very impressed. Thanks for the stuff. She's in her bed now talking to the mermaids." I point towards the hallway knowing full well she's going to want to tell Arianna goodbye. This isn't going to be easy for her I'm sure.

***

"You're going to stay with your Dada tonight sweet girl. I'll be upstairs if you need me ok? You sleep tight and I'll see you in the morning." I give Arianna a kiss and hold her tight. My heart is breaking but I know they need to do this tonight. A part of me hopes she can't make it very long but the other part of me hopes she does.

"Wuv you." Arianna says and kisses my cheek breaking my heart even more.

"I'll come get you in the morning okay?" I blow her a kiss and walk out the door and back into the living room where Jonathan is.

"She'll be fine ya know." He smiles and pats the couch cushion next to him.

I shake my head no and walk to the door instead. But before I can open it I say, "I'm right upstairs if she needs anything. I don't care what time it is either."

"We have you on speed dial. Everything will be just fine. Don't worry." He smiles and puts a hand on my shoulder. If my head and insides weren't already in a jumbled mess, they sure are now.

"Please call me if you need anything."

"Don't worry, I will. We're going to make some dinner, take a bath and sleep in her new big girl bed. We'll be fine."

"Okay. Like I said I'll be upstairs if you need me."

"Why don't you go out with some friends? Enjoy your time alone without having a toddler to take care of? Go see an adult movie. Go get a drink. Whatever you want to do."

"I'll think about it but doubt it. Take care of her." I point at him with a stern look on my face.

He nods and I walk away leaving my heart behind. How do I deal with this?

Maybe going out and not being alone in that apartment is what I need. Hmm.

I'll call Zandra. She's a fellow artist that sometimes comes around to paint with me. She's always trying to get me to go out with her.

That's what I'll do.

"Hey yep it's me. I was hoping you were free tonight. I need to get out and do something to take my mind off of Arianna spending the night with her dad. Yep I'll be ready and I'll fill you in. See you in a few. Thanks Zandra."

I rush into the apartment and straight to the far right portion of my closet. The portion that holds all those sexy going out dresses that I used to wear so frequently before Marianna got sick.

Wow that feels like a lifetime ago.

I feel almost giddy while choosing the dress, shoes and jewelry for the rare night out.

Thirty minutes later I hear a knock at the door. My first thought is panic that something is wrong with Arianna. I throw the mascara tube down and grab my purse before rushing to the door.

"What's wrong? Is she okay?" I say as I swing the door open.

I'm struck by the sight of Zandra being there in a short silver dress instead of the hunky soldier I had envisioned.

"Wow you've got a lot of explaining to do Missy."

"Yes there's A LOT I need to tell you. But I need a drink first. Or a couple even." I lock the door and follow her to the waiting limo.

"Limo? What's this about?" I stop and look at her like she's lost her mind.

"It's not every day my friend Lizzie calls and wants to go out. I called in a few favors and got us transportation for the night. Neither one of us has to drive. Now get in." I see her get in the back door where a man that I assume is the driver is standing holding it open. Before I know it she's standing up hanging out the sunroof too. She's being so loud I catch a couple of the neighbors looking out their windows.

Then I see the one person who is occupying most of my brain open his door and step outside smiling.

"Hey. I see you took my advice. Wow you look amazing." He says looking me up and down.

"Yes, I called my girlfriend Zandra who is always wanting me to go out with her and I guess she thought it was a special occasion!" I say motioning towards the limo.

"Well you'll knock all the guys dead with that dress and those heels. Have a good time." He turns to go back inside but not before turning his head one more time to look at me.

I smile and wave knowing he's shocked to see me all dressed up like this. I can't help but feel amazing seeing how he reacted to my appearance.

Oh shut up Lizzie. He's just shocked to see you in something other than jeans. Get a grip.

"Let's go gorgeous! The night is waiting!" I look up at her and smile. I can do this.

"Thank you." I step into the limo and instantly feel happy and very excited for what lies ahead of us.

This. Is. Going. To. Be. A. Great. Night.

***

Wow I can't believe my eyes just saw Lizzie looking so smoking hot! Whoa.

And I'm not so sure about her going out clubbing or whatever with that woman that was barely wearing any clothes at all. Men are going to flock to their sides but not to talk to them that's for sure.

Why did I suggest she go out tonight? I could have had her stay here instead. She could have slept in my bed and I could have slept on the couch.

Okay that brings another visual in my brain. Lizzie in my bed. Wrapped in my sheets. WHOA! Jonathan this is not helping.

I decide it's time to cool off and not think about how amazing Lizzie looked or how good she smells every day.

I crack the door of Arianna's new room and sigh when I see she's out like a light snuggled up tight with the pink teddy bear I gave her the first time I met her. Wow. My heart swells and I'm not so sure it's not going to burst.

Looks like tonight's going to be just fine. Maybe I should get some rest myself in case she wakes up and can't get to sleep. Doesn't look like Lizzie's going to be home any time soon if we did need her.

I shake my head thinking what an idiot I am that I suggested it to her in the first place. Way to go idiot.

Just as I'm ready to settle in I hear my phone beep on the nightstand from getting a text message.

Everything okay? Just checking in.

Lizzie. She's been gone forty-five minutes and already worrying. She's not enjoying her time away as much as I had thought.

I smile and decide to ignore the text hoping she'll get back to what she's doing and not worry. Maybe she'll think we're asleep and relax. I'll take a cold shower, that should help me to relax.

A few minutes later I'm stepping out of the bathroom and can hear my phone ringing nonstop.

I was wrong. Very wrong. My phone hasn't stop going off for the past ten minutes. I see about twenty texts and three missed calls. All from the same person.

Lizzie.

"Hello?"

"Jonathan!! Is everything okay? You haven't responded to any of my texts or calls. I'm so worried!"

"Lizzie calm down honey it's all fine here. We were sleeping. Arianna's in her new bed zonked out and I was actually in the shower. Sorry I didn't mean to worry you."

"Oh my goodness I was so worried. I was ready to literally run home on foot if I needed to."

"No, you stay and have fun. She is just fine and asleep."

"Oh well ok. I guess I'll let you get back to um. Showering. Or sleeping."

"I'm going to bed now. I'll see you in the morning. Have a good time. But behave." I say smiling trying to visualize Lizzie doing anything but behaving.

I've got to get to sleep and quit thinking about Miss Goodie-Two-Shoes. Although she didn't look so innocent in that short dress and sky high heels.

Whoa. Maybe another cold shower would be better.

14

"We need two shots of anything you've got that's going to make someone forget their own name." Zandra tells the bartender at the first bar we get to.

"A shot? Probably not the smartest idea. I haven't drank in a long time and I'm not sure I can tolerate too much."

"You'll be fine. I've got this." She hands me a small glass with clear liquid inside. It looks like water but we all know it's not. I take a deep breath and let it out.

Here goes nothing. "EEEEKKKK that's nasty! It's burning all the way down Zandra! Are you trying to kill me?" I spit and sputter trying to recover from that disgusting tasting poison.

"Well, it'll loosen you up I promise. Let's go dance."

"You are a whirlwind aren't you? I can't keep up with you."

"We need another drink. Not a shot don't give me that look. A big girl drink that'll help drown the nerves you're suffering from."

"Now that Jonathan finally answered my call and I know she's okay I'll be fine."

"He was so freaking hot Liz. Oh my goodness.. Hot soldier man candy."

"Whoa tiger. Down girl." No way does she have a shot with him. Just no way.

"You're a kick. I have sure missed this!" She clinks her glass against mine for what I assume a one sided toast. I smile and shake my head at this crazy wonderful friend. I'm actually very happy that I came out tonight. Very glad.

"Oh, I love this song. Let's go dance!" She pulls me onto the dance floor and it feels like I'm trying to learn to walk again. I feel so awkward and stupid. That is until I get this sudden surge of energy and courage. Must be the shot. At least it's good for something. I look over at Zandra and see that she's enjoying herself not worrying about how dumb she looks so I guess I can do the same.

I start to feel the music and let it talk to me. I'm not sure if the moves look like they feel but the way they do feel is amazing. It feels almost like I'm free for the first time in forever. I guess I kind of am.

"See now this isn't so bad is it?" She wraps her arms around me and hugs me tightly.

"You know, I'm feeling great thank you! You're the best!"

"We need to do this more often!!"

"Yes we sure do." Heck this might be all I do once Jonathan takes Arianna back to Oklahoma with him. Maybe I'll become a partying lush that never has to feel the pain.

Yuck no way. I'm stronger than that and he promised he wouldn't leave until we both agreed on it. And we are far from agreeing right now.

"Turn the brain off Lizzie. Look at that hot specimen across the room. He's hot!"

I look over my shoulder trying to see who she is talking about and about fall over myself when I realize that it's my ex-boyfriend Tanner. Holy crap I haven't seen him since I broke up with him when Marianna got sick.

I try to hide myself behind Zandra but it's too late. He's spotted me and headed our way.

"Oh he's headed our way. I call dibs on this one sweetie." She looks at me and pushes me towards the edge of the dance floor.

She's going to be so disappointed when she finds out I already had dibs on him years ago....

I continue to walk off the dance floor praying to every God possible that Tanner won't come after me. My prayers were definitely not answered when I feel an arm go around my waist from the back and get pulled against the front of another human body. A very male human body. Weirdest part was I could recognize this human without even seeing him. The feel of his arm and the smell of his cologne triggered memories that I probably shouldn't be having at this moment.

"Where you think you're going Liz?" I feel a hot breath against my ear before I hear the words. The sensation from him being so close actually sent shivers through me. There always was a good amount of attraction between myself and Tanner. He just wasn't on the same page as I was when it came to my sister and niece.

"To sit down. I'm tired and thirsty. Zandra will dance with you if you want." I try to step out of his grip but I'm a fool to think he'd let me go after all this time that easily.

"I would rather talk to you. I haven't seen you in forever." He spins me around and gives me a friendly hug. As soon as I put my arms around him I have a perfect view of a very upset friend. I smile a shaky smile and mouth my apology. She just huffs off and finds another available man to dance with.

I feel terrible but what was I supposed to do?

"Ok let's find a table somewhere a little quieter." I say and start to search for one. I'm a little shaky at the moment so sitting down would be best. The attraction I had for Tanner hasn't dissipated over the years. That's for sure. And mixed with the alcohol and high heels, I'm in way over my head.

As we walk to the only open table left in the entire establishment, I feel Tanner put his hand against the small of my back. It's almost like it's never left. My heart beat has to be going a hundred miles an hour and I'm praying he can't see the way I'm reacting to his nearness.

"You haven't changed much Liz. I was so shocked to see you and I had to watch for a few minutes to make sure it was you."

"Zandra wanted to come here tonight so I decided why not? What are you doing here? This has never been your scene either." Or maybe he's change more than I can visibly see.

"My cousin Marcy is in town from New Jersey so I told her I would hang out with her tonight. Little did I know she was on the hunt for a man." He laughs and it's so good to see him happy and laughing.

The last time we saw each other it definitely wasn't under these easy going circumstances. I had decided to take care of Marianna and ultimately take care of Arianna and he wasn't ready to be that tied down so we parted ways.

"So, what's been going on in your world since we last saw each other?"

"Working. I started that sporting goods store we had talked about and it's been doing so well we've expanded to a couple of different locations in Charlotte. I work mainly in the corporate office though."

"So you really did it? That's awesome. I'm so proud of you and happy it's working out so well." I honestly feel that way too. Tanner is such a great guy and I loved being with him.

"And you? How did everything turn out for you?" He's afraid to look at me. Is he still upset with me for breaking it off with him?

"Well, Marianna had a little girl named Arianna. Unfortunately she passed away a while ago so I'm trying to raise her myself."

"Oh I'm so very sorry to hear about that Liz. That's just tragic."

"Are you upset with me for breaking things off with you when I did?"

"Oh goodness no. I'm actually very ashamed of myself for being such a selfish jerk and not being there for you when you needed someone the most. I wasn't sure you would even talk to me tonight when I first saw you." Looking down again. So that's why he is afraid to make eye contact with me when talking about my life.

"Tanner I don't blame you for not being ready to take on a baby and my sister's cancer drama. Believe me I never held any ill feelings about you for it. I knew it was going to be tough. I am so glad to see you went on and did what you'd always dreamed of. I really am proud of you." I lay my hand on top of his. He looks at our hands then rolls his over which allows him to wrap his big hand around mine. He's now holding my hand and actually looking at me.

"Lizzie you were the most important thing in my life but I just didn't feel like I was going to be able to help with your sister or be able to help raise a baby. I have never gotten over you or stopped loving you either. I've thought about you almost every day of the past couple of years." He's now rubbing circles on the back of my hand with his thumb.

With every circle my body seems to relax even more. Tanner always was such a calming presence.

"Oh Tanner. I wish I could say the same but I've had so much going on and so much to deal with that I've barely thought of anything other than Marianna and now Arianna. I have missed you though. It's so great to see you and talk to you now."

"I completely understand. The worst has happened and you've

overcome every bit of it with grace. You're my hero Liz." This time he lifts my hand and kisses the top of it. He pauses and looks up at me before removing his lips from my hand. That makes me feel so safe. Nothing like the butterflies I feel when Jonathan touches me but a good feeling either way.

How can two different men make me feel so different? It doesn't really matter because I can't have either one. Especially not Jonathan. Tanner doesn't want me either, heck I'm not even close to the girl he used to love. Yes I know he says he still does love me but I'm not the same Liz he knew back then. And then there's Arianna. She's part of the package and he was clear when he said he didn't want kids.

"I'm flattered believe me, I just can't think about it all too much. I can't let myself get emotional about it because I have to be strong for Arianna. She's the one who lost the most in all this."

"You lost just as much. You knew her mother a lot longer than she did. She won't even remember her. You always will. Am I right?"

"Yes but I still can't let myself fall apart. Especially now." I must have let the stress from the whole situation with Jonathan flash across my face because Tanner scooted his chair closer to my side.

"Lizzie I want to be here for you. I know I said I didn't want that before but I'm a changed person too. I've done all I set out to do and even though I got all of what I wanted, something is missing. That something is you Liz." Tanner is now running the back of his hand down my right cheek. My heart just jumped in my throat.

"You don't know what you're saying. You've had too much to drink and it's the alcohol talking." I shy away from his touch now and try to scoot away but he grabs the back of my chair and holds it in place.

"No. I am sober as an ox. I haven't had one drop. I'm drinking club soda so that no one realizes I'm not drinking. I have to take care of Marcy tonight so I'm the DD."

"Tanner I really don't know what to say here. The last time we talked you didn't want a family and now I'm a package deal. I have a little girl that I have to think of too."

"And I want any and all of you. I told you I still love you and when I saw you from across the dance floor I knew you were the missing piece of my life's puzzle. Yes, I know that sounds extremely corny but it's true."

"Tanner. I've had too much to drink for this conversation. Jonathan's here and I'm not sure how long I'll even have Arianna. It's all too much."

"Jonathan?" He asks leaning back just a bit unsure of where this is going.

"He's Arianna's birth father." I see his eyes get large and eyebrows raise.

"I thought Marianna didn't have any contact with him?"

"She didn't. But before she died she had a P.I. find him and sent a letter explaining all about Arianna and gave him my contact info if he wanted to see her. Well, he called and he's now living in an apartment in our building so he can be near her and get to know her. That's where she is tonight. Their first overnight."

"Oh Lizzie that's got to be eating you alive. Are you okay honey?" He squeezes my hand in support.

"I've texted a few times but she's sleeping just fine and not phased at all. She instantly had a connection to him when they first met and it's been growing stronger every day."

"What's his story?"

"He's from a small town in Oklahoma but he just got back from a deployment. He literally just got back and the letter hit him the same day."

"Wow. A soldier then? You'll have to tell me the whole story sometime. Maybe lunch tomorrow?" He starts to smile at me and as I look into his eyes I see the love he professed earlier. This guy really does love me. There isn't pity in his eyes like most men have when they first hear the story. There's actual admiration and love in them.

Maybe I can do this. Maybe this is why I was sent here tonight. Maybe this is what my life is heading towards. Tanner. Hmm.

"I think that would be great but can we maybe do breakfast instead? I'm not going to want to leave Arianna again after I finally get her back."

"Breakfast it is. She can come with you if you want. I won't mind meeting the sweet little thing."

"Maybe another time."

"Ah yes we probably need to take it slower than that huh. I'm sorry, not trying to push."

"It's okay, really. I'm glad you have an interest in meeting her but we need to get to know each other again before you do."

"Got it. I have really missed you Liz." This time he's leaning in for a kiss. At first I panic and think about pulling back but I can see Zandra over Tanner's shoulder giving me a big smile and thumbs up. Oh what the heck!

I meet Tanner's lips and the second they touch I can feel the emotions stirring again. The kiss is great don't get me wrong but it's definitely not like kissing Jonathan. Jonathan? What the heck am I thinking of him right now for? There's an actual hot blooded male in front of me wanting a part of my life and I'm thinking about the one who doesn't? What is wrong with me??

"Well my dear it's almost midnight and we need to get you home. The limo is mine for about thirty more minutes. You ready?" I hear Zandra say from behind Tanner which causes me to jump back from the kiss. He smiles at me and stands introducing himself to my friend before saying goodbye to us both.

She is standing there with her hands on her hips smirking and says, "Seriously girl? How do you have two of the hottest men in town fawning all over you?"

"Two men fawning over me? What on Earth are you talking about?" I honestly have no idea what she's been into but I do not have two men after me.

"This ex and the new ex-soldier. You knew exactly who I was talking about. Don't play dumb. You are far from it." She reaches over and grabs her purse from in front of me.

"You don't know what you're talking about. Tanner's the only guy even remotely interested in little old me."

"Uh huh that's why Mr. Hot Soldier came outside and about swallowed his tongue when he saw you in that get up!"

"Oh whatever. He was curious at the ruckus you were making like the rest of the complex." I reach into my purse and check my phone to make sure Jonathan hadn't called or texted me.

"And you're only checking that phone out of worry for the baby. Keep telling yourself that Lizzie. One of these days you might believe it. Let's go." And she marches to the front entrance and is outside before I realize which way she went. I am still standing there shaking my head when she comes back in and gives me the look like 'what are you still doing in here?'.

"Coming mother." I smile and follow her out the door this time.

15

I have seriously looked out these front windows of the apartment a hundred times since it started to get late. Lizzie hasn't come back yet that I have seen but I'm really starting to get worried about her.

I should have never encouraged her to go out with her friends. What was I thinking? Especially looking as hot as she did. Whoa.

"Dude you really need to get out of the front window and get some sleep. Arianna is fast asleep and you should be too." I check the lock on the door for the millionth time and force myself to not look out the window.

I walk to my bedroom and lay down. Looking at the clock on the night stand I see it's a little after midnight and I just can't believe she isn't home yet. Maybe I should text her to check in? No she'll think something is wrong and freak out. Dang I just need to sleep.

After tossing and turning most of the night I'm groggy the next morning and don't even realize there's a little body in my room. That is until I open my eyes to see another pair of them directly in front of me.

Having never had someone staring at me in my sleep before, I jump back and scream making the curious little person in front of me jump and cry.

"Oh angel don't cry. You scared me. I'm sorry I scared you too."

I pick her up and cradle her in my arms with my heart melting the instant she lays her head against my chest. I feel her start to relax and stop crying and know that this is what I want to do every morning.

"How about some pancakes? Does that sound good to you angel?"

"Yay pantakes." She smiles and gets excited.

"Ok let's go cook us some grub. Lizzie might show up soon too. Maybe she can have breakfast with us. Ya think?"

Arianna just smiles and tries to get out of my arms. I take it as a sign that she wants down to play. "Ok you play with your toys while I make some pancakes."

I look at my phone a little curious as to why Lizzie hasn't called or texted yet about coming to get Arianna. I figured she would be at the door the minute the sun came up. Heck maybe she's not even home yet. That thought doesn't make me very happy. Hmmm.

***

"Thank you for breakfast Tanner. It was great talking and getting to know you again." He grabs my hand as I get out of his car. I smile up at him a little taken back by how touchy feely he is. I'm definitely out of practice in that department.

"It was a great time. I would like to take you out again if I could. I want to spend as much time with you as I can. I don't want you to get away from me again." He squeezes my hand and smiles.

I feel myself sigh in total teenage girl style. Geez. One guy gives me attention and I turn into a teenager again. Wonderful.

As we walk towards the stairs I hear my name being called by a little voice. I instantly turn around excited to see her.

"Arianna sweet girl!" I run over to where Jonathan is walking with her along the sidewalk. I see him looking at Tanner like he's got four heads. Oh boy.

"We thought we heard your voice but we didn't realize you were just getting home."

"Oh no we had breakfast this morning. I was home about 12:30

this morning. Um, Jonathan this is Tanner, Tanner this is Jonathan. Arianna's father."

"Nice to meet you." They shake hands and mumble the same pleasantry. Neither one seems to feel the words though. I look at Jonathan and he's actually pretty ticked off it looks like.

"Has she eaten?"

"Of course she has. It's almost 11 o'clock Lizzie."

"That was a dumb question I'm sorry."

"She was only asking a question. No need to snap at her." Tanner says and glares at Jonathan. Oh crap this isn't going well.

"Look I'm going to take Arianna to the pool in the complex, come join us if you want. We'll be back later." Jonathan takes Arianna back and gives me a look of disappointment or something I'm not real sure of.

"He's pleasant. No wonder you're so worried about losing her."

"No, he's a very nice guy. I think he was just surprised by you being with me."

"Why? Does he want to be with you?"

"Oh no. We're trying to be civil you know until the decision needs to be made about Arianna."

"Well, if you need anything you can always call me. I'll have your back no matter what." He leans over and presses his lips to me softly.

"Thank you Tanner that means the world to me. I had a great morning and I've enjoyed getting to know you again."

"She's adorable by the way. And she sure loves you."

"I love her so much it hurts. It's like she's my own child, not my niece."

"I can see that. It's great to see you with her. You're a natural."

"Thank you Tanner. I would like to spend more time with you if you're interested."

"More than interested. When are you free again?"

"Tomorrow night Jonathan can probably take Arianna again if you want to see a movie or something."

"Any time I can spend with you I'll take. I will talk to you later Liz. I have missed you. Missed us. And definitely missed this." And he leans over and really lays one on me. Wrapping his arms around my waist he draws me close. I get lost in the kiss and wrap my own arms around his neck hearing a little sigh that had to have come from me.

"Until next time my love." Watching the man I used to love walk away again makes me have mixed emotions. I do have feelings for Tanner but I'm not sure that the passion is what it should be. Not like with someone else I know. Grr! Stop thinking about Jonathan!

I stomp into my apartment and quickly change into a bathing suit before stopping in the bathroom to take a quick look at myself. I'm startled to see that I'm smiling and I'm really not sure I've smiled like this in a very long time. I need to give Tanner another chance because maybe now we're meant to be together. Hmmmm. Could we be?

I walk to the pool area and stop dead in my tracks when I get close enough to see the most magnificent male body I've ever laid eyes on. Holy crap he's amazing. And that smile as he plays with Arianna makes my heart leap out of my chest. Whoa down girl.

***

I'm laughing and playing in the pool with Arianna trying not to obsess over watching for Lizzie to come join us. I'm also praying she doesn't bring that sorry excuse for a man with her. I know I don't really know the guy so I shouldn't be saying that. I don't think I could handle watching him put his hands on Lizzie let alone when she has a bathing suit on. If she comes at all. She may have decided to stay back at the apartment with 'lover boy'. Ugh that makes my skin crawl and my stomach drop.

As I toss Arianna up once more, I catch the sight of something I never dreamed I would see; Lizzie standing there at the edge of the pool in a two piece blue bathing suit. A bikini, what else did I expect? She is gorgeous, I am so taken with Lizzie that I about miss catching Arianna. I hurriedly walk to the edge and sit her down, as I do she sees Lizzie coming towards us and screams, "Mama swims?"

Lizzie and I both look at each other stunned. Neither of us knows what to say to her.

"I'm going to swim with you, is that ok?" She looks at me with eyes that are also asking the same question of me.

"Will you go with Lizzie and I'm going to go get some work done at the apartment." There is no way I can stay here with Lizzie looking like the most beautiful thing I have laid eyes on. I don't know what I was thinking inviting her.

"Are you sure? I don't mean to intrude." Now she looks upset.

I put my hand on her shoulder and we both freeze again. Her bare shoulder. Her skin is so warm and soft. Holy crap I am going to have to get out of here before anyone sees the affect this woman has on me.

"Nope I need to get busy and I'm sure you two need some time alone. I'll see you later. Bye baby I love you." I kiss Arianna on the forehead and hurry back to the apartment, and I mean hurry.

***

Did that seriously just happen? Did he walk away like I was the plague? Geez do I look that hideous? I thought this bikini would be the best choice, but I guess I should've put on a smock instead. I can't believe he just left.

"Well, baby girl, do you want to stay swimming while we're here, or do you want to go have a snack?"

"Snack, please!"

"Ok, let's go get a snack, and try to forget about your dad. Boy! I don't know what I am going to do about him Arianna." I take Arianna out of the pool and we walk towards the apartment, as we turn the corner to where we see Jonathan's apartment I see that his doors and windows are shut, the blinds are even shut. I wonder if he's even inside? And why did he run away from me? I can't be that bad.

I don't know, maybe the look in his eyes were not disgust, maybe it was, oh, maybe he thought I looked hot! Hmmm.

"Let's just figure this one out Arianna. Come on; let's go see what your dad is doing." So we turn left instead of right and head towards Jonathan's apartment.

Knock, knock, knock.

We wait.

Knock, knock, knock.

We wait some more.

Knock, knock, knock.

"Baby girl, do you think he's in here? Hmmm he isn't answering. Guess he really didn't want to talk to us. Let's just go to the house." So we walk back to our apartment and as I shut the door I see in the mirror that I don't look like a three horned scary monster. I wonder what his problem was and where did he go? Oh well, on with my life I guess. I should call Tanner, maybe that was what I needed to do, was call Tanner and just forget all about Jonathan. Jonathan, Jonathan. He's taken hold of my whole life, my mind, my everything. What am I going to do now?

***

I get back to the apartment and I don't know what I'm supposed to be doing here I want so badly to go back to the pool. Lizzie looked so hot I couldn't even think straight and I can't let her know she affects me.

Can I?

No, she has a boyfriend. Ugh, Tanner. Well, I can't just stay here so I'll go work out. I've got to do something to get this restless energy out. Ok, well, on to the gym we go.

After being in the gym for what feels like hours. I'm dripping with sweat and completely exhausted but I feel amazing. My muscles and body are screaming at me louder than my mind. Mission accomplished. Now for a shower and some sleep. This time I may actually be able to sleep.

I walk back to my apartment but can't help looking to the stairs that lead to Lizzie's and as I do Tanner is walking up the steps with flowers and a giant teddy bear. Seriously, is he trying to buy my daughter now too?

I am seeing red! Lizzie may not be mine, or even a possibility, but that little girl is all mine!

Wow, she really is all mine. There is nothing holding us back from leaving. Huh, especially now that Lizzie has this moron hanging around. She shouldn't fight me on Arianna going to Oklahoma anymore. Hmmm, do I start those legal proceedings or not?

And here I thought I was going to be able to sleep tonight. Ok, maybe not.

16

I have bathed both myself and Arianna, while also succeeding at finding both of us a snack, but Jonathan hasn't left my thoughts. Where could he have gone? Surely he doesn't have a girlfriend that I don't know about. Maybe that's why he left so fast from the pool. He must have had a date.

Why does that thought make me feel so badly? "He is not yours Lizzie, get over it! You could also get serious again with Tanner, he sure wants that, but do I?"

On one hand Tanner and I feel right. We got along great before and I do still have some lingering feelings for him, he's easy on the eyes and definitely seems to feel the same about me. I guess all that's left is to see how Arianna and Tanner interact without Jonathan around.

Jonathan, ugh! Why does this have to be so hard? What if he is ready to get custody of her now? He definitely has that right. Then he and this new girlfriend could go back to Oklahoma and take Arianna with them. Oh my goodness I would be all alone if that were to happen. What would I do then? How do I go back to being a single woman without a niece to take care of? Wow that feels so wrong. I'm not sure I could handle that.

Knock, knock, knock.

That sound breaks me out of my thoughts and Arianna squeals while running to the door.

"Dada, Dada." She yells as we open the door. We're both surprised to see that it isn't Jonathan.

"Tanner? What are you doing here?" I see Arianna frown and walk back to her room disappointed.

"I was thinking about the two of you and decided to show you. These are for you and the bear is for Arianna." He hands me an amazing bouquet of red roses and a very large white bear.

"Oh, Tanner this is too much, but thank you." I smile and awkwardly try to hug him with all these gifts in my hands.

"Nothing is too much for you, Liz. I want you to know how serious I am about you."

"Let me put these in water and get Arianna." I turn and take a deep breath letting it out slowly. It's now or never to find out how they'll get along.

After putting the gorgeous roses in a vase I head to Arianna's room where I find her playing with the pink teddy bear that Jonathan gave her.

"Hey Arianna, there's someone I want you to meet. Can you come out to the living room with me?" She nods and takes my out stretched hand.

I lead her to where Tanner is waiting. He smiles, stands and picks up the bear again.

"Arianna, this is my friend Tanner, Tanner this is Arianna." Tanner walks towards us but kneels right in front of her.

"Hi, Arianna, it's so good to meet you. I brought you this bear. I hope you like it."

"I have bear from Dada." She walks back to her room. Oh goodness that wasn't a good start.

"I'm sorry Tanner. I'm not sure she knows how to accept another new man into her life right now. Can we just take it slow? Please don't take it personal."

"Don't worry I'm ok, she's had a lot happen to her and isn't sure how to accept more. I'll win her over just like I am going to do you. I'm confidant." He presses his lips to mine and I feel some of the tension drain away. Maybe this is the guy for me.

"Not Dada, not Dada!" Arianna yells suddenly as she pounds her tiny fists into Tanner's legs. He looks at me with shock at the sight of a little human beating at his legs.

"Arianna! What are you doing? You know better than to hit people." I lean down to pick her up trying to calm her down.

"Not Dada, not Dada! He not Dada!" She continues to yell, visibly growing angrier by the second.

"Tanner please give me a second." I take Arianna to her room and shut the door behind us. Sitting down on the bed, I situate her so that she is able to see my face and me hers. She looks so upset and I don't think I have ever seen her this bad. Her face is all red and her eyes are bloodshot from crying, the poor baby is even shaking. It just breaks my heart to see her like this.

I pull her tighter against my chest. "Arianna, what is going on? Are you ok?"

She pulls away from me and looks directly into my eyes. This time her eyes are clear and determined.

"That no Dada, you no kiss, he no Dada."

"Honey what do you mean?"

"He no Dada, no kiss" she says with more sternness.

"I can't kiss Tanner because he isn't your Dad?"

"No!" she lights up with the answer but makes me even more worried.

"I don't kiss your Dad either Arianna." Ok that is kind of a lie, but it was only that one time and she never saw that.

"Yes, kiss Dada." She is getting agitated at me again.

"Arianna, your Dad and I aren't going to be kissing. Tanner is my friend and he might be more soon. I want you to be nice to him. He wants to be your friend too."

"My friend?"

"Yes, do you want to go back out there and say 'hi' to your new friend?" She nods and pushes off of my lap but waits for me to leave the room as she follows behind.

Tanner stands once again when we enter the room with a questioning look on his face. "Everything ok ladies?"

"Arianna is ready to say hi to her new friend Tanner."

"Hi, Tanna." She says the words, but does not look up.

"I brought you a bear, do you want it now?"

"No, have Dada bear. You take." She points to me.

"Ok, I'll take the bear. Thank you Tanner."

"Me go play?" She asks while looking up this time but only at me.

"Sure, say goodbye to Tanner though."

"Bye" and she runs to her room shutting the door behind her.

"Baby steps Liz, baby steps." He wraps his arms around me as I lay my head against his chest and I realize that Arianna thought Jonathan and I were together. What would have given her that idea? She didn't see us kiss that one time, or even see us close enough to kiss. That is so strange.

"Earth to Liz, where did you go?" He kisses my forehead and I feel myself relax a little. It feels so good being comforted by a man again. Feels good to feel wanted again for sure, I could definitely get used to this. I just pray Arianna is going to be ok with me and Tanner.

"I'm just worried about her. She was so upset because she thought I should only kiss Jonathan. He and I aren't together and there's no chance of that happening either. I just don't understand where that came from."

"It's ok I'm sure she just related your situation to what she sees around her and on T.V. Most kids' parents do only kiss each other. She's confused, but it'll get better, I promise." I smile at him and lift my lips up to his.

"You are so wise."

"Liz, I didn't expect to come back and have everything be storybook perfect. It won't all happen in one day, as long as you're willing to try then I'm good."

"Of course I'm willing to try! I would be dumb to let someone like you go again!"

"Things are much different this time Liz, I'm 100% ready for it too." He lowers his head and kisses me tenderly and then not so tenderly. I can feel the heat start to elevate the kiss while he pulls me close. It seems like forever before he pulls away, both of us breathless.

"You do that to me every time, Liz. Next time I may not be able to stop. I'm going to go this time so it doesn't bother Arianna. Next time she's staying overnight with her Dad, call me." He kisses me once more before leaving. Leaving me speechless and confused.

17

"Hey mom, how are you? I'm great. Yes, she's amazing. That's actually what I'm calling about. How would you like to come and meet her? I did buy a pick up here so I'll be able to come and get you in Charlotte. Ok, that's great. You're going to love her Mom. I do. Of course she'll love you too. You're her only grandma. Ok, let me know when you get in. Love you. See you soon."

Not fifteen minutes after I hang up the phone with my mom there's an e-mail from her with the flight information. I would say she's excited to come meet her new granddaughter. That makes me smile. I better warn Lizzie, but I think I'll just send a text since Tanner was last seen going up the stairs. With my luck he's still there. Grrr.

My mom's coming tomorrow for a few days FYI.

That should do it, now do I have mom meet Lizzie too or just Arianna? I guess I'll leave that up to Lizzie. I don't have to wait too long for her reply.

Ok let me know when you need me to keep Arianna if at all while she's here.

Didn't figure she'd want to be around. She'll probably be gone with Tanner the entire time. That moron will always make me frown. I'm going to need Botox for my frown lines at this rate.

***

His mother! Seriously, how do I deal with her now? What if she doesn't like me or she thinks I'm not doing a good enough job with Arianna. She may talk Jonathan into leaving for good with her and taking his daughter with him. Oh goodness this feels like the worst idea ever but I type back a reply anyway.

Ok let me know when you need me to keep Arianna if at all while she's here.

There, that way I'll have no reason to be around his mom. He can just bring Arianna by whenever he needs to and I'll stay hidden here in my apartment. She's coming to meet Arianna, not me. No one will know the difference if I'm not there.

Do you want to meet her? She wants to meet you.

Oh crap, so much for staying hidden. Just tell him no and you're too busy Lizzie you don't have to do it.

Sure let me know what your plans are for her visit.

Way to stay strong you push over, now you're stuck meeting his mother. This is not going to be good.

"Hey Zandra I need help, Jonathan's mother is coming tomorrow and she wants to meet me. Yea, I know, I need help picking out appropriate clothes. Paint covered overalls are all I own."

"Alright, I'll be there in a minute. I'll bring my rescue kit."

"That is exactly what I need, rescued!" I breathe a sigh of relief knowing the cavalry is on its way. Zandra will have me mother-meeting-ready in no time, if that is even possible.

Knock. Knock. Knock.

"Right on time" I say as I open the door, but as I do it looks like a circus is in town and all filing into my living room. Oh boy, here we go.

***

"I'll go pick up Mom in Charlotte and be back as soon as I can. Ok, when I get back can you bring Arianna over to the apartment?

She might need you close when she first meets Mom and that way she can meet you too. Sound good?"

"Yep, let us know."

I hang up the phone shocked by the short answers. Something is definitely off in Lizzie's voice this morning. Driving to Charlotte I'm left with nothing but confusion where Lizzie is concerned. What do I do about Arianna? Can I live here forever? I don't really want to. I want to be around my family and friends. I want my daughter growing up knowing she is loved by many. But how do I take her away from Lizzie? I can't do that, either. She would never go with us while Tanner's hanging around. This is hopeless, no matter what decision I make someone will be hurt. My only hope is that Lizzie will move with us to Colvin. Maybe my Mom can help with that. Gosh I hope they get along ok. This can only get worse if they don't.

***

"Hello?" Good grief who now? I answer without even looking at the screen.

"Hey Liz, I was wondering if you and Arianna want to have breakfast with me and go to the zoo."

"Wow, that sounds great, but Jonathan's mom flies in today. He's actually gone to Charlotte to pick her up."

"That should take a couple of hours; don't you think we have time?" I look at my watch for reassurance.

"Ok yea, you're probably right. No reason to sit around here waiting for doom."

"Doom?"

"Yes, I'm not too excited to meet her. What if she hates me and encourages Jonathan to move with Arianna?"

"No one can hate you Liz, you'll win her over like you do everyone else."

"Well, thanks for the vote of confidence, but I'm still not sure about this."

"I'm down stairs, so get Arianna loaded up and meet me at the stairs. We'll get you out and your mind off the whole mom drama."

"Ok, be right down. Wait, you're already here? What were you going to do if I had said no?"

"I was confident you wouldn't." See, even he knows you're a push over Lizzie.

"See you in a few."

That crazy man, is he really that crazy for me? Doesn't this all seem so sudden? I guess not with our relationship before. We don't have to start from scratch, right? Am I making trouble again where there isn't any? Of course I am. Isn't that what I do?

I rush around getting Arianna and I ready for the zoo. Before we step out the door she finally realizes we're leaving the apartment.

"Going?"

"We're going to the zoo for a bit today. Doesn't that sound like fun?"

"Dada too" She says excitedly.

"No honey, we're going with Tanner."

"Why no Dada?" she whines out. Oh great, here comes the hissy fit again.

"He went to pick his mom up at the airport, your grandma. You'll get to meet her later."

"Dramma?" This poor kid is learning all kinds of new words and people that go along with them.

"Yes, grandma, not sure what she will want you to call her though."

"Dramma. Dada. Dramma. Dada." Oh good grief she's never going to shut up now. I smile at the sound of her excited voice. I could listen to her chatter on all day. Except when it's about her Dad. I could do without that I guess. Get used to it Lizzie. Ugh.

"Ready for the zoo?"

"Yea, Dramma, Dada waiter?"

"Yes, let's go, Tanner's downstairs waiting to take us to see some animals." And just like that she forgot all about the grandma drama. Finally. If only it were that easy for me.

"Wow! You look amazing Liz. When did you get your hair cut?"

"Zandra came over last night and helped me to get ready for Jonathan's mom's visit."

"Why did you have to change anything for them? You're perfect just as you were." He is a little upset over this. Interesting.

"Tanner, I felt as if I needed a little change. Why is that so wrong? A lot is riding on whether this woman likes me or not. I could lose Arianna if she doesn't."

"Liz, I talked to my buddy Rob and he looked into your situation.

He said with Marianna leaving you custody of Arianna when she died, that you have just as many rights as he does."

"You talked to an attorney about this? I never asked you to butt in."

"Liz, I was only trying to help you, trying to ease your mind. Please don't get upset."

"Upset? I am furious Tanner! I already have an attorney and I don't need another, so butt out!"

"Whoa, ok, ok, ok, I never expected this reaction from you. I'm sorry for overstepping." He really does look surprised by my reaction. He honestly thought he was helping. Now I feel like a lunatic.

"Ugh, I'm sorry, I just unloaded on you. I'm stressed out about this and I totally took it out on you."

"Liz, I know honey. That's why I talked to Rob, but I won't do that again. I mainly asked for me, if we're going to do this then I needed a little help figuring out what I'm looking at with Jonathan and Arianna."

I walk up to him and wrap my arms around his neck, when he looks down at me I sigh and say "We're in this together."

"Together, I like the sound of that. Let's go see some animals for a while." He kisses my lips lightly before opening the car door.

"Yes, let's go."

18

"Hey Mom, it's so good to see you."

"Oh honey I have missed this handsome face." she says with a hand on each side of my face.

"I'm so glad you could come for a few days."

"Did Arianna come with you?"

"No she's with Lizzie until we get back."

"Oh I was hoping she'd be with you."

"You'll see her enough when we get back. Lizzie's letting her stay with us as much as we want."

"Letting her? You're her father Jonathan; you should be able to spend however much time you want with your child, without needing her aunt's permission."

"Calm down mom, that's not what I meant. I meant that she told me to let her know if I needed her to watch Arianna any time while you're here."

"Oh so you didn't have to ask to have her?"

"Not at all, Lizzie assumed I would want to have Arianna as much as possible while you're here."

"Well, maybe she isn't so bad after all."

"Not at all; she is an amazing person and very attached to Arianna."

"You like her don't you?" She says with an ornery grin.

"Mom, no match making, she has a boyfriend."

"You didn't tell me that when you were home."

"It's new, apparently they dated before Marianna got sick and they couldn't make it work back then."

"And now they're trying again?"

"Guess so."

"You really like her!"

"Mom, please!"

"It's just an observation; let's go meet my granddaughter."

"Yes, let's go."

***

"Tanner this was a great morning; thank you for thinking of us."

"I am always thinking of you Liz."

"Oh Tanner you're good for my ego."

"I'm serious Liz; you are all I can think about."

"Well, while Arianna is gone with Jonathan the next couple of days why don't you come stay with me?"

"Are you serious?"

"Of course; it'll be a good time for the two of us to be alone."

"That sounds like Heaven Liz. I'll drop you two off and go home to pack an overnight bag."

"That works, but how about I let you know after she leaves."

"Sounds like a plan."

We pull up to the apartment building a few minutes later and as we get out of Tanner's car I can't help but scan the parking lot for Jonathan's new pick up. I don't see it, thankfully.

Tanner clears his throat to get my attention and I look at him questioningly.

"Doesn't look like they're back yet, you're safe for now." he smiles and kisses my forehead.

"Looks like it. I'll let you know." I kiss his lips quickly and usher Arianna to the stairs and then the apartment. I'm not looking forward to these next few hours.

"Look what you've got me into Sis, thanks a lot!" I look to the Heavens and frown.

***

"Well, Mom we're here; home away from home."

"It looks like a very nice place son. You said Lizzie lives here too, right?"

"Yep, that's why I chose here. I'm close by for Arianna."

"And you're close by for Lizzie too." She smiles and gets out of my pick up.

"Mother." She waves me off and starts towards the sidewalk.

"Which is yours my boy? I am a bit tired."

And that is the end of that conversation, for now anyway. I smile with the thought of mom not changing at all over the years. She's always been a force to be reckoned with and clearly still is. But the matchmaking is going to be a tough one to stop.

I take out my phone and hit Lizzie's contact. "Hey, we're back but Mom wants to rest for a little bit before we have Arianna come down."

"That's good because she's napping anyway. I'll let you know when she wakes up."

"Thank you Lizzie, see you then." She didn't sound as irritated as she did earlier. That's good, right? Women, I don't know.

"Lizzie is going to bring Arianna down after she gets up from her nap."

"Sounds good, I'm going to go unpack and rest myself."

"Ok I'll run to the store and get some stuff to get us by for the next couple of days."

"You're such a good boy. You're going to make some woman very happy someday. Someday sooner, I hope."

"Mother that was five minutes without you match making. That's a new record for you."

"Love you son, wake me when that beautiful girl of yours is here."

"Ok I can do that."

"And her gorgeous aunt that has you in knots." She smiles wide and hurries into the spare bedroom.

"Mother." I say as I roll my eyes. Good grief, maybe I don't want her meeting Lizzie.

***

"Hey honey, are you ready to go meet your new grandma? She and your daddy are waiting for you to wake up."

"Dada? Dramma?"

"Yep, are you ready"

"Yay!"

"Ok you get your teddy bear and I'll let them know we're heading down."

I quickly walk out of the room desperate for somewhere out of her line of sight where she can't see me panicking. I'm far from ready for this meeting. Taking deep breaths and letting them back out slowly help to calm me enough to allow me to text Jonathan.

She's up and we're headed your way.

Not even a second later I get his reply. Geez is he waiting by the phone or what?

Ready here, we will see you in a few. =)

He must be excited because he ended that with a smiley face. Seriously, I wish I felt that way; my emoji would have a green puking face.

Ready or not here we go.

I send as a text to Tanner and get his instant reply also. They say women live with their phones attached to them.

Go knock 'em dead Liz. <3

A heart emoji, what is up with these two males today?

19

Knock. Knock. Knock.

"Hey Lizzie, Arianna come on in." Jonathan answers and catches Arianna as she jumps into his arms.

"Dada, Dada"

"I missed you too baby girl. Did you have fun at the zoo with Lizzie?"

"Tanna."

"Oh, he went too, how nice." I can feel him looking at me, but I'm keeping my eyes down to the ground.

"Mama pet graff, tongue yucky."

"I pet a giraffe today and she didn't like its long tongue."

"She's been calling you that a lot more here lately."

"Yes, and I honestly don't know what to do about it."

"I'm ok with it if you are. She doesn't even remember Marianna and you're the closest she has and will ever have."

"Really? I figured your new girlfriend would want that position."

"What girlfriend? That's news to me."

"Oh I thought since you left the pool in such a hurry the other day and then when we came to your apartment and you weren't there. I thought you had a date."

"Um, no I was at the gym, no girlfriend."

"Well, ok, umm, I'm sorry for assuming. Can we get this over with? I'm very nervous."

"I can tell, but why, it's just my Mom."

"That's exactly why. If she doesn't like me she could influence you to leave with Arianna."

"Lizzie, I told you I'd never just rip her away from you."

"I know, but you have the opportunity to ruin my life and there's really nothing at all I can do about it."

"Lizzie relax, my Mom just wants to meet you, no judgment."

"No judgment at all, I just want to meet the woman who did anything in her power to take care of my granddaughter after her Mama passed away." We both jump a little while Mom smiles mischievously.

"Mom, you could have told us you were there."

"Nonsense I walked in and heard your conversation. Now, I am Ella Mae Doone, so nice to finally put a face to the name and a very pretty face if I do say." She looked at Jonathan and smirked. If I didn't know better I would think I saw him blush, surely not.

"Lizzie, well Elizabeth Kentis actually, please call me Lizzie. Very nice to meet you, I have to admit I've been scared to meet you, but that was silly. Right?" I say the last part looking at Jonathan who is standing next to his mom holding a squirmy Arianna.

"Well, now that the awkward is over, how about we get back to the task at hand."

"Right, Mom this is Arianna. Arianna this is my Mom Ella Mae."

"Dramma!" and she lurches herself to Ella Mae's open arms.

"She called me Grandma. Oh little one I have been praying you would want to call me that. You're such a gorgeous little thing."

"I tried explaining who she was coming to see, I hoped you wouldn't mind her calling you Grandma."

"Of course not, I love being called Grandma. As soon as my kids were grown and ready to have children of their own, I looked forward to being Grandma."

"You have a gorgeous set of granddaughters if I do say so myself." Jonathan says beaming at Arianna and his mom.

The sight of Jonathan introducing his daughter to his mother makes me miss my Mom a lot. She'll never get to meet Arianna or any other grandchildren she may have.

"Thinking about your own Mom?" I'm shaken out of my daze by a deep voice. I look up at its owner and feel as if I'm going to faint. How can one person make me feel so much from a single question and a look?

Tanner, I have to think of Tanner he's here for the taking, not Jonathan. It would be best if you'd remember that Lizzie.

"I think it's time for me to go and let you all have some time to get to know each other."

"You don't have to Lizzie."

"It's ok, Tanner and I have plans anyway enjoy your visit and take care of our girl. See you soon. It was very nice to meet you Ella Mae."

"You have plans? Really? That must be why you look so amazing, your hair looks really good and Tanner will love that pink dress for sure."

"Umm, thank you? Have a good night, bye baby girl." I kiss her forehead and slip out the door walking to my own apartment in a fog. I feel so many emotions right now. Jonathan said I look amazing. I wasn't sure he even noticed the changes, but Tanner did as soon as he saw me. Why am I so confused between those two? One is available, one isn't. No contest, so why am I struggling with this whole thing?

"Grrrr!"

***

"No wonder you're still here, she's spectacular and she feels the same way about you, Son."

"Oh whatever Mom she has a boyfriend and left to be with him, not us. Your match making radar is on the fritz."

"Not so fast Jonathan, I know what I'm talking about. The way she looks at you is the same way Karlie looks at Aiden. And exactly the way you look at her."

"Can we change the subject now?" Clearly irritated I say and walk away. I cannot do this right now. That woman gets to me every time I'm around her and apparently it's obvious, just great.

"Are you ready for some dinner?" I say to Mom and Arianna once I come out of my room and cooled down.

"What are you making us? Are you hungry sweet baby?" Mom's got Arianna sitting on her lap all cuddled up like they've known each other all along.

"See, she knew you were family the instant she saw you."

"She's a smart girl and my goodness doesn't she look like your sister?"

"That's what I said when I first saw her too. I was afraid to upset Lizzie, but wow they are like twins."

"Yes, Lizzie said she always thought she looked like Marianna, but when I showed her the picture of Karlie she couldn't help but agree."

"It's crazy that this little girl who looks just like your sister has existed here all this time and none of us had a clue."

"It is, but I'm just thankful that Marianna's P.I. found me. I wish it would have been sooner, but it is what it is."

"God sent her to you when you were ready and able to be her father. If you would have known before you were back in the States it wouldn't have changed much."

"Very true, it still kills me to think of those three dealing with all of that alone, while I was living a single man's life."

"You were a soldier Jonathan not exactly living it up in a world of violence and sand."

"True again, but now Lizzie is terrified I'm going to take off with Arianna."

"Well, Son you do need to figure out custody and where your home is going to be, especially before she starts school."

"I know without a doubt that I want to take her back to Colvin and raise her there."

"But…."

"But I know it'll crush Lizzie."

"Talk her into going with you! Problem solved."

"Why would she want to go with us? Her life is here."

"Arianna is her life."

"True again. Where have you been all this time?" I smile and hug her tight.

20

"I know without a doubt that I want to take Arianna back to Colvin and raise her there."

"What? I knew it! How could I think he wouldn't do that to me?"

I came back to bring Arianna's blanket that she forgot and overheard Jonathan's confession from the front window. How could I have been so stupid? What am I supposed to do now?

I quickly reach for my cell phone once I get out of view of Jonathans apartment and call Tanner.

"I need you please hurry."

"Honey, what's wrong?"

"Please just hurry!" and I break into hysterical crying rushing back to my apartment.

I open the front door, shut it, and slide down into a crouch sobbing uncontrollably. My world just came apart.

Knock. Knock. Knock.

"Liz. Honey, are you in there?" I hear from behind me so I stand up and slowly open the door. As soon as I have it opened a crack, Tanner throws himself inside and wraps me up in his arms.

"Baby what is wrong, what happened? Do I need to go kick his butt now?"

"No, just hold me."

"Anytime Lizzie."

After what felt like hours I pull away from Tanner and start to explain all that had happened and what I ended up overhearing.

"Oh, Liz I'm so sorry. I know this is exactly what you have been afraid of happening."

"I don't know how I'll ever go back to being alone here. For that matter, I don't know how I can be alone anywhere."

"You'll never be alone again Liz, I'm here and I love you."

"Oh, Tanner" I start to cry again and like last time he wraps me up in his arms and lets me fall apart.

"Feeling better now?" Sometime while I was sobbing, he had picked me up and carried me to the couch.

"I think so, as good as I can knowing I'm losing Arianna who's been like my own daughter all of her life."

"Honey, I know. We can have more too if you want."

"What? Have more what?"

"We can have more little girls for you to love so much, we could start our own family."

"Replace her? Are you serious?"

"I never said replace Liz, I said start our own."

"I do want more kids, but how do I even think of that now?"

"Honey I know you don't want to hear this, but Jonathan is her father. Her mother died and left you in charge of your niece. It might be time to let Arianna go with him and live the life she's meant to and you move on with yours. You'll still be a part of her life as her aunt. He wouldn't do that to you."

"I know every word you say is right, but it hurts so badly to think about not having her around anymore."

"I know Love, you're too good to be true. You're the best thing to ever happen to me Liz. I was going to do this at a later date, but maybe now is the right time." He gets off of the couch and kneels on one knee in front of me and I gasp. So shocked I'm speechless. Is this really happening?

"Elizabeth Kentis you are the most amazing woman I have ever met and after I lost you once I vowed that I would never lose you again. I know this is sudden but I know all there is to know about you already, so why wait? Will you marry me and let me love you for the rest of your life?"

"Tanner, oh my goodness, I can't believe this. I never dreamed this would ever come. I don't know what to say. I do have feelings that never went away and you are an amazing man. You're great to always think of me first."

"Is that a yes, or a no?" He looks scared.

"Yes, of course yes. I would be a fool to let you go again. I could never find anyone who treats me better than you."

"Great, I think. I know things are messed up right now, just know I'm always here for you."

"Thank you, I love you too by the way." I do, don't I? Isn't that right? It isn't just as a friend is it? Of course not Lizzie, you have known Tanner for a lot longer than the other man you're trying to not think about right now. I just need to stay away from Jonathan; that should help me keep my love life straight. Right? Easy. If only I believed myself.

***

"Lizzie we're going to the park today. Do you want to go with us? I'm sure Arianna misses you."

"Thanks for asking but I'm not home anyway."

"Oh, um, I'm standing next to your car, so I thought you were."

"No, I'm with Tanner, but I'll come see her later, after her nap. Is that ok?"

"Sure, see you then."

She's with Tanner again, that seriously makes my stomach churn and my blood boil!

"What did she say Honey? Is she going with us?"

"No she's gone with him."

"Oh, that's what the murderous look is on your face." She smiles. Really? How is this amusing?

"Let's just go. I need to get out of here." I storm to my pick up and get in the driver's seat, letting mom handle situating Arianna into her car seat.

"Son, you need to talk to her."

"Talk to her about what? She's free to do what she wants."

"Your feelings."

"My feelings? Why do I have a feeling you're going to clarify what those are?"

"You really can be obtuse sometimes. You like her, maybe more than like."

"No, not going to happen, she has a boyfriend and I need to focus on my daughter."

"Ok" She shrugs in defeat. Or surrender. Ugh!

"Wow, that's it, just ok?"

"Let's just go enjoy the day."

"You don't need to tell me twice." I say under my breath.

***

"Who was that?"

"Jonathan, they're going to the park and wanted me to go."

"Did you tell him you were with me picking out your engagement ring?" Tanner says with the biggest grin on his face. Why don't I feel as joyous about this engagement as he does?

"Nope, I just told him I was with you. I probably need to tell him that we're engaged, but I need to tell him that news in person."

"Maybe so, but you're going to tell him, right?"

"Of course I am Tanner. I can't really get married without him knowing."

"Do you want me to go with you when you tell him?"

"No, that might make it worse. I'll tell him this afternoon when I swing by after Arianna's nap."

"Here's your ring, do you like it?" He slips an unimaginably beautiful ring on my finger.

"It fits perfect and it's amazing, how could I not like it?"

"You don't seem as excited as I am about this Liz."

"I am excited; I'm just worried about the whole Arianna situation." I wrap my arms around his waist and lay my head on his chest. I've got to learn to mask my unease better than this. Tanner doesn't deserve to see how mixed up I am right now.

"I love you Liz." He leans his head down and kisses the top of mine.

"I love you too. Thank you for my ring, it is truly amazing." Who wouldn't love a ring with a diamond the size of their knuckle? Geez, this is so unreal.

21

"This is the place I met Arianna and Lizzie for the first time Mom."

"Oh, really? I can't imagine how different it must be to be back here without Lizzie, and knowing Arianna now."

"Seems like a lifetime ago."

"Are you planning on coming home anytime soon? Your sister is dying to meet Arianna."

"I know, I'm just not sure what to do yet."

"Are you ready for a nap sweet girl?" She says as she snuggles Arianna.

"No."

"It's time anyway, one more time down the slide." I say and walk her up the stairs.

"You've settled into the Daddy role quite well."

"Well, I learned from the best, Mama."

"Your Daddy was so great with you kids."

"I miss him so much."

"Me too Son, I miss him too. He would be so proud of you for stepping up and being here for your little girl."

"I wouldn't want it any other way, even as confusing as everything is, I cannot imagine not being here with her."

"Definitely not ideal, but you'll do what is best for Arianna."

"I'm trying." I watch Arianna go down the slide and squeal with joy as Mom scoops her up at the bottom.

"Are you ready to go sweet baby? Grandma needs a nap too."

"Naptime for you and Grandma."

***

"How was the park? Did you go down the slide?" I ask Arianna after her nap. I walked down to see her as soon as Jonathan told me she was awake.

"Swide fast!"

"I bet you did, how are things going?" I ask Jonathan hoping to fill the awkward silence. I know I need to tell him about the engagement, but I'm not sure how to tell him. I don't know how he has managed to miss the rock on my finger.

"You have some new jewelry there Lizzie." His mom noticed, great.

Well, here we go, it's now or never. I look at Jonathan "Tanner proposed to me last night."

She takes my hand for a better view of the ring. "Wow! That is some rock you have there, girl."

"It is beautiful, yes, I'm just not sure I'll ever get used to the feel of it, I hit it on everything."

I see Jonathan's face turn red before he stomps out the door.

"Where is he going?" I ask his mom.

"Um, I am not sure."

"Oh boy, I'll be right back. I guess I better go talk to him."

"Sure, I'll stay here with Arianna."

I slowly walk outside in search of Jonathan. I don't see him for the longest time, but then see him sitting on his tailgate.

"Your small town boy is showing." I say when I see him sitting there legs swinging back and forth.

"Your gigantic rock is showing." He says angrily.

"Are you mad at me?"

"No, I am not mad, shocked, yes."

"Why would this shock you and make you mad?"

"You just started seeing him, how can you be engaged?"

"Jonathan, we have known each other for years."

"I guess I'm just shocked it happened so fast." Jonathan says as he rolls his eyes and shakes his head.

"Why does it matter? He'll never take your place with Arianna."

"Oh, I know that. Um, sorry, I just thought that we….well, never mind."

"You thought we, what?" Is he trying to tell me that he thought we were going to have a shot? Surely not!

"Never mind, I'm happy for you, if you're happy."

"I am happy….it's a little strange, but I guess I'm happy."

"You guess? Geez Lizzie. Congratulations then."

"Thank you."

"Well, I guess it's time for me to figure out what to do with my life too." After a little bit of awkward silence.

"I can't help but ask, are taking Arianna back to Oklahoma now?"

"I have thought about it, yes."

"What is stopping you?"

"You, but now that you're getting married; there's no reason to wait." What the heck does he mean I have stopped him from leaving?

"Me?"

"I didn't want to leave you here alone." Well, of course that is all it was, I should have known it was nothing more. But I can't help feel my heart melt a little too.

***

"I didn't want to leave you here alone." Liar, you are a big fat liar.

"But now you're just going to leave with her." She says flatly.

"I guess so, what else am I supposed to do?"

"Well ok." She jumps off the tailgate and runs to her apartment. Women are so confusing. It was as if she was almost not happy about her own engagement. Almost like she did not want to be marrying Tanner, but she is. Dang, this is not what I wanted to happen, but I guess I'm free to take my daughter home to Colvin now.

Home. It's strange how Oklahoma doesn't feel as much like home anymore, at least not without Lizzie.

"You ok, Son?" I hear from beside me as I turn to see the two most important females in my life.

"I'm fine, let's go home."

"Home?"

"Colvin." I get down and shut the tailgate before I take Arianna from Mom's arms.

"Let's get her home where she belongs."

"Ok, I'll get you two on my flight for tomorrow."

"Great, I'm going to go get dinner started." She puts a hand on my arm and stops me.

"Are you sure about this Jonathan?"

"Yep, I should have done this from the beginning."

"Before you fell in love with Lizzie, you mean?"

I roll my eyes at her. "Yes Mother, now drop it ok?"

"Deal, let's go home."

"Hmm, home."

***

Of course I cried my eyes out on the way to the apartment, but I also know there's nothing I can do to keep him from taking her. She belongs with her dad, not her aunt; even if she does feel more like my daughter than she does my niece.

I'm sitting here on her bed, with my knees pulled up to my chest just looking around at the empty bedroom when I hear the door.

Knock. Knock. Knock.

"Please don't be Tanner or Jonathan; I can't deal with them right now." I sigh and walk to the door and start to open it, but when I do I'm completely taken back at the sight.

"Ella Mae, what are you doing here? He's not leaving right now is he?"

"Can I come in for a moment, Lizzie?" Duh Lizzie, she's still standing outside.

"Of course, I'm so sorry."

"Don't apologize Lizzie, you're overwhelmed right now with emotions."

I pick this exact moment to bust out into hysterical tears again; this is getting out of control.

"Let it out sweetheart." Ella Mae says as she holds me. When did that happen?

I break away and look at her. How can she be so nice to me?

"I am so sorry about that, I'm sure you're here to get Arianna's things. You're not here to listen to me cry."

"It's ok; I actually came to check on you. Jonathan said he told you about going home tomorrow."

"Tomorrow, my goodness he moves fast!" I try not to break down again, but I can't believe she's leaving so soon.

"I'm afraid so. They're going to fly home with me."

"What about his pick up?"

"He'll fly back later to get all of Arianna's things and drive it back to Oklahoma."

"So, I guess I need to pack her some more stuff."

"Could I help? You shouldn't be doing this alone. Why don't you call your fiancé?"

"Tanner? Oh, um, well, I haven't gotten the chance to call him yet."

"He should be here with you Lizzie; you shouldn't be alone right now in this frame of mind."

"I know but I just can't call him."

"Are you sure about marrying him? My daughter Karlie was over the moon when Aiden proposed to her. She would tell anyone or anything that would listen. That is all she talked about until the wedding and you just don't seem happy about this."

"Honestly I am so confused."

"You can talk to me if you need to Lizzie. Just because Jonathan is my son does not mean that I can't be objective."

"I really wish my Mom or even my sister were here to talk to right now. I just feel so alone."

"I'm sure you do miss them now more than ever."

"Yes, and I'm going to miss Arianna so much. She's the only family I have left." Tears start to fall from my eyes again.

"Oh, Lizzie dear, you're a part of our family now too. We owe you so much for taking care of Arianna selflessly all of this time."

"I couldn't have let anyone else take care of my sister's little girl."

"And now you have to. I understand, but he's an amazing man and he'll take care of her. All of us will."

"He is yes, and I know you all will that's the only thing making any of this bearable."

"You're welcome to come to Colvin anytime you want."

"Are you sure it's a good idea to have any contact with Arianna?"

"She's going to miss you dear; I think she's starting to believe you're her Mother."

"She does believe that, doesn't she?"

"Like I said, here is my address and phone number at home. Call me anytime and come to visit as often as you can. There's no need for you to just disappear out of her life; you're still a part of her family."

"Thank you Ella Mae, can you help me to get some of her things packed up?"

"Most definitely."

"I don't know how I'm going to be able to say good bye tomorrow."

"To Arianna or to Jonathan?" I look up at her stunned at her perception of all of this.

"I guess both, if I'm going to be honest."

"He cares about you too Lizzie. You could always come with us."

"Come with you? That would never work out. Jonathan and I aren't together and of course there's Tanner."

"You have a lot to think through."

"I guess I do."

We pack Arianna's little suit case until it's ready to bust at the seams.

"Well that's all of it for now. I'll get the rest packed up and have it ready for him when he comes back for his pick up."

"Remember what I said, take care Lizzie." She gives me another tight hug.

"Thank you. Good night." I shut the door feeling even more confused than before. How in the world could Ella Mae think that I would go with them? I would love to of course, but that would never work. How could that work? He doesn't want me around. He wouldn't be going back to Oklahoma if he did, right?

22

"You ready?" I look up at Mom from where I've been standing against my pick up.

"Yes and no, am I doing the right thing?"

"Yes, she needs to be home where Karlie and all of us are. You need the support system too."

"I know, but what about Lizzie? This is going to tear her apart."

"She'll be fine."

"She has Tanner, I know." I frown again.

"I was going to say she's strong but has a lot to think about though."

"Why, what all did you say to her last night?"

"Nothing you need to worry yourself about Son. Let's get the last of our bags and go before we miss our flight."

"I wanted to give her more time to say good bye though."

"Quit worrying."

"Sorry, that's easier said than done."

We walk back to the apartment where Lizzie is inside saying good bye to Arianna.

"Well, that is all of it." Lizzie looks up at me with red swollen eyes. That is definitely a shot through the heart. I don't want to hurt her, that's the last thing I want to do. I want nothing more than to gather her small body up in my arms and never let her go.

"Well, sweet girl, I have to tell you good bye so you can go with your Daddy and Grandma. You get to fly on a really big airplane."

"Airpane, Airpane."

"Yes, you're going to have so much fun but I'm going to miss you so much. I love you." She leans over and kisses Arianna on the forehead and I see her body quiver as she's trying so hard to hold everything together.

"Momma go?"

"No, I'm staying here and you're going to your new home to meet more of your family."

"Momma cry?"

"No, I'm ok. I'm so happy that you'll be surrounded by so many people who love you."

"Me wuv momma. Dada, momma go?"

"No baby girl, Lizzie is staying here."

"I love you so much Arianna, call me after you get there ok?"

"Otay, wuv momma."

"Please take care of her Jonathan."

I can't take it any longer and pull Lizzie into my arms and hold her tight.

"You know I will, you take care of yourself Lizzie."

"I will, have a safe trip." A tear slips from her left eye, knowing it's all going to blow; she turns and runs up the stairs to her apartment.

My heart shatters into a million pieces knowing how much I'm hurting her. I can't do this, I just can't do this to her. I turn to look at Mom to tell her I can't when I see Tanner pull up beside us. At that point reasoning overrides my emotions. She has him, she doesn't need me.

"Let's go." I can't doubt my decision any longer.

"Have a safe flight." I hear him practically singing to us. That man just won the jackpot and it makes me dislike him even more. I vaguely hear Mom reply to him, but I know if I even look at him I'll lose the control that's just hanging by a thread.

"Is everyone in and ready to go? Let's blow this popsicle stand."

"Popsicle?"

We all laugh, which allows me to swallow the uneasy feeling and focus on the task at hand.

Good bye Lizzie. Take care of her Tanner, you don't deserve her. I don't deserve her either I realize as I start my pick up and drive away.

***

"Honey, are you in there?" I hear Tanner knocking on the front door; I really need to get him a key.

I walk to the door and open it, knowing I must look like a total mess.

"Oh honey, come here, I tried to get here before they left, but traffic was awful."

"She's gone, gone, just gone." I start to sob again, this time not caring who hears or sees me falling apart. My heart is beyond broken.

"I know Liz. I know, it'll all work out. I'm here for you. You're not be alone, I promise."

"Alone? I will forever be alone without Arianna." No matter how much Tanner is here, he can never fill the void that just formed inside of me. "I'm going to go take a bath, make yourself at home."

"Ok, I'll be right here when you get out."

I mumble something that I'm not even sure were words and take one step after another to the bathroom. I step inside, shut the door and see Arianna's bath toys in the bottom of the tub.

"How am I supposed to do this, she is everywhere that I look. I can't live here anymore; I cannot bear to be here without her." I stand up, splash cold water on my face and open the door determined to not fall apart again.

"Liz, that was a quick bath, what's going on?"

"We have to go, I'll move into your house. I just can't be here without her."

"Um, ok, but what about your stuff?"

"I'll hire movers to come get it all. I just can't be here. I have to go."

"Well let's go then."

We walk out of the apartment for the last time that I had shared with Marianna and then only Arianna, but it's not our apartment anymore. It's just me now. Just me forever.

"I'll meet you at your house. I'll need my car at some point."

"Are you sure Liz, we can come back for it."

"No." I shake my head and get in my car shutting the door to stop anymore dialogue with Tanner.

Pulling away from the building, I look in the back seat one last time knowing she's not there. Knowing she'll probably never be back there again. I sigh and vow to never look back, at least today.

23

"Watch for your sister, I'm sure there's a gigantic sign too."

"I wouldn't put it past her." I chuckle while scanning the crowd of people around us as we exit the plane in Tulsa.

Arianna fell asleep ten minutes in the air and hasn't woken up since. I smile and hug her tighter loving the feeling of her cuddled close in my arms.

I look right one more time and see a huge sign with letters in all caps.

JONATHAN & ARIANNA.

There's the sign. I think Arianna's is written in purple with glitter, imagine that. Never underestimate my little sister. Too bad Arianna's asleep, she would love it.

"There she is and has a sign, I'm so shocked." She teases and waves at an overly excited Karlie. She's jumping up and down like a child while Aiden is standing there shaking his head.

"Hey sis, I'm glad you didn't cause any kind of a scene." I joke and hug my sister the best I can while still carrying Arianna.

Aiden shakes my hand and says, "She wanted to yell as soon as she saw you, but at least I put a stop to that."

"He's a party pooper." Karlie pouts and punches Aiden in the arm.

"You're embarrassing in public sometimes." He says wrapping his arms around her and kissing her on the forehead.

"And she's the embarrassing one? Get a room, would you?" I joke and reposition Arianna. "She's getting heavy, so can we get a move on please?"

"You'll get used to the numb arms after a while." Aiden says and takes the bags from our hands.

"Thank goodness for wheels on suit cases! I don't know how we could have done all of this without them!" Mom says winded.

"I should have gotten a stroller for her, chalk this one up to inexperience."

"It'll all come together big brother. Do you want me to carry her for a bit? I really wouldn't mind." Karlie beams up at me and bats her eyelashes.

"Gladly, I think she gained twenty pounds on the trip."

"How long has she been out?"

"The whole flight; I was afraid it would hurt her ears, but she didn't even notice." Mom says this time handing me the suit case handles.

"She did very well for her first time on a plane." I say proudly.

"She's a Doone, of course she loves flying." Karlie says as she kisses Arianna's sleeping face a few times.

"Yes she is, let's go. This grandma is exhausted and ready for a nap."

We all chuckle and head for the car. I'm surprisingly overjoyed to be back in Oklahoma with my family and having my daughter with me makes it even better.

***

My stuff should arrive today from the apartment. Just my things though, I had them box up anything that had to do with Arianna and put it in storage.

I'm anxious to get my things put away here at Tanner's house, so at least it'll feel a little like home for me too. Right now it just feels as if I am on vacation and staying at a friend's house.

"I'll be home before three today so I can help get your things inside, will that work?" Tanner says as he ties his tie. He stops and looks at me expecting a reply. Except I'm standing at the window looking out at the unfamiliar view lost in my own misery.

"Honey, are you ok?" I startle as his arms go around my shoulders and pull me up against his chest. This simple gesture of caring should make me feel better, but I'm so numb it doesn't even faze me.

"I'm sorry, what?"

"Liz, are you ok, honey?"

"I'm fine; just thinking about a new painting that I need to get working on for a client." I lie. If he believes that line of bologna, then I should become an actress in my spare time.

"Ok, well I was saying I'll be home by three to help move your things inside where you want them."

I nod and smile; there's not much else to say here. There's really not much else I can say at this point about anything. I'm floating through my days in a fog, more numb than I have ever been before. This feels worse than when Marianna died. I guess then I had Arianna to take care of and didn't have time to fall apart.

Now I'm here with neither one of them. Maybe I'm mourning the loss of Arianna and Marianna now. Geez that is messed up Lizzie, because you know full well that you're mourning the loss of a sexy soldier that you kissed only one time, but haven't been able to get out of your system since.

Now we're getting to the real issue; not only am I upset about losing Arianna and our home, but I have also lost any and all chances that I might have let my imagination dream up with Jonathan. Oh come on Lizzie, this is so not fair to Tanner. You agreed to marry him and here you are thinking of Jonathan.

I am beyond messed up. This is ridiculous. "Ugh!"

***

"Here we are; home sweet home." Mom says as we walk through her front door.

I'm once again carrying a sleeping Arianna while mom pulls the suitcases behind her.

"It feels so good to be home." I say comforted by the familiarity of the house I was raised in.

"You can put her down in Karlie's old room for now if you want."

"I've got to look for our own place soon."

"Nonsense! There is no reason for you to move somewhere else with Arianna when I'm here in this big house all by myself with empty bedrooms everywhere. You can keep your room and we can fix Karlie's room up for Arianna."

"Mom are you sure about this? You already raised your kids and I don't want you to think you have to raise mine."

"Jonathan Gene Doone I think no such thing! You and that little girl need all the love and support you can get right now. You'll need to work anyway so I could watch her here at the house without disrupting her any more than we already have."

"When did you have time to come up with the answers to everything?" I smile and hug my mom feeling my heart swell so big it feels as if it'll burst.

"Now go lay Sleeping Beauty down." I nod and walk to Karlie's childhood bedroom.

After I get Arianna all settled in, I take our suitcases to my room. I smile at the difference between my black suitcases and Arianna's purple ones with pink hearts. Never in a million years did I think I would have a child that would be here in this house with me.

"Unbelievable." I say to myself.

I can't help but wish Lizzie's things were among ours and how awesome it would be to have her here with us too. I could come home from work to find her fixing dinner with my mom and we could both get Arianna ready for bed each night. Then once we were able to go to bed ourselves…

Whoa! Where did that come from? Good grief you've got to get a hold of yourself you idiot. Nothing good can come from those ridiculous thoughts! I shake my head and open my suitcase determined to get unpacked and never go down that thought path again.

***

Shouldn't they be there by now? Why hasn't he let me know? I pace back and forth in Tanner's living room, well my living room too, I guess. The movers called about a half hour ago saying they were going to be here by 2:30 PM. I look at the clock to see it's only 1:45 PM which gives me enough time to call and check on Arianna. Or should I not? Should I wait for him? Surely everything went okay and he's just busy getting her settled. And there's probably a ton of family and friends swarming their house.

My mind instantly conjures up the picture of Jonathan being surrounded by beautiful women wanting to fill the wife and mommy roll. That makes me want to scream! No one is supposed to be her mommy but me since Marianna died! How could he just replace me like that? Ella Mae said he cares about me. If that were true he wouldn't be holding interviews!

Whoa what the heck was that all about? You don't even have a clue what's going on there and you're so worked up over nothing. I don't know what is happening to me; maybe Tanner needs to lock me up for a while. I'm acting and thinking completely insane!

I throw myself down onto the couch and cover my eyes with one of my arms. I need to find a way to move on from all of this crazy. Once my art supplies are here I can throw myself into work and hopefully that'll help. I can only pray it will.

Knock knock knock.

I'm jolted awake suddenly not realizing I had fallen asleep. I look at the clock on the wall to see it's almost 3:00 PM.

"Oh goodness, hope I didn't miss the movers!" I say and hurry to answer the door.

"Ma'am are you a Lizzie Kentis?"

"Yes sir, I am."

"I believe we have a truck load of stuff that belongs to you."

"Oh thank Heavens you do!" I hug the scruffy guy making him look at me strangely.

"Well where would you like it all? In a storage unit or just inside here?"

"All in here please. I can direct you as you bring it in if that works."

He nods and heads back to the moving truck and waiting crew.

After what seems like hours, the last of my things have been brought inside Tanner's apartment. I once again look at the clock to find its 4:45 PM now.

"I thought he was coming home before three to help?" I mumble to myself and begin a search for my paints, brushes and canvases.

24

After unpacking all the suitcases, I start towards Karlie's room to check on Arianna but Mom stops me before I can reach for the doorknob.

"She's fine. I just checked on her. Have you called Lizzie yet?"

"No. I've been putting it off because I don't want to hear the hurt in her voice."

"She's probably waiting by the phone wondering if we made it safely."

"Yes you're probably right. I'll call her." I pull my cell phone out of my back pocket and scroll for Lizzie's name. As I get to it I see the snapshot I had chosen as her contact picture. It's one of her and Arianna smiling at each other. Longing and guilt hit me so hard it about knocks me over.

"Just hit send. It's not going to call for you. Or would you like me to call her?"

"Would you?"

"Yes of course." She takes her phone off the kitchen counter, taps the screen a couple times and lifts the phone to her ear. Look how simple that was you moron. Why couldn't you do that?

"Hi Lizzie. Just wanted to let you know we made it to my house safely. Yes she did wonderful. Actually she's been asleep since takeoff. Jonathan's getting her settled but I wanted to call and let you know we were here. Are you doing okay honey? That's great news. Oh yes work will definitely help. Okay well, you remember what I told you last night. Take care sweet girl, bye-bye." She hangs up and turns to look at me. I can't tell from her expression what she's thinking.

"Well?"

"Well what?"

"The call. What did she say?"

"She said thanks for letting me know." And Mom walks to her bedroom leaving me standing there like a fool knowing that conversation was more than that. Women!

I stomp back to my room and shut the door before texting Tarley.

Hey man. Home in OK now. FYI

I send the update hoping he'll call me once he reads it; wanting more info. He always wants the scoop on everything.

Nice.

That's it? What is going on with everyone right now? I guess that's what I get for being a coward and not calling her myself. Now nobody will talk to me.

***

"Hello Ella Mae! Thank goodness. How did she do? Did she sleep at all? Thank you for letting me know. I've been worried sick. I'm fine, well as fine as I can be under the circumstances. I've moved in with Tanner. My things got here today. I've been working on a client's painting since then. Okay I will. Thank you again. Goodbye."

She has got to be the sweetest woman ever. I'm so relieved to know they made it okay and Arianna slept the whole time. How funny; that girl would sleep through a hurricane. I smile remembering how soundly she always slept through summer storms. Don't go there Lizzie. Keep focused on work, Janet wants this painting next week and it'll take you day and night to get it ready. Just what the doctor ordered.

I'm startled out of my groove when I hear someone knock on the wall beside the door. I look up to see Tanner standing there with his arms crossed and not looking very happy.

"I didn't hear you come in."

"I'm sorry I didn't make it back by three like I said I would." He steps toward me reaching out his hands for me to take his but as I start to reach for them I look down at my hands and see the paint all over them.

"Hang on. Let me wipe this off first. What time is it anyways?" I look around for a clock and wipe my hands clean as I do.

"11:30." He frowns.

"At night?" Unable to believe him myself, I hit the button on my cell phone. Sure enough, the screen displays 11:38 PM.

"I'm sorry I'm so late." He kisses my forehead and walks out of the room without another word. I'm still standing here in shock that it's almost midnight and he just now came home. Does this happen all the time?

***

"Hey sis, what's up? I was hoping Arianna and I could come out to the AK today. I think she's getting restless being cooped up with me and Mom all day."

"Of course, come out now and the girls can play before lunch."

"Okay you're a Godsend. See you soon." Maybe getting us out of the house for a few minutes will help calm everyone's nerves.

"Mom we're going to run out to the AK for a while. We'll be back for naptime, most likely."

"I think that's a great idea Jonathan. I'm going to run to the shop and see how Nancy's doing with the new orders. Then I'll come back and finish packing up Karlie's things from her room. Maybe I'll run by the thrift store and see about some more toys."

"Okay thanks. But if you need to be at the bakery please don't let us keep you from it."

"It's fine. That's why I hired Nancy. She can run the shop just fine. Now you go."

"Okay if you say so. I think Arianna needs to run around with Aleah and forget she's in a new place."

"For sure. It'll get better Son, I promise. Her whole world's been turned upside down and we just need to get her a new routine. Things will calm down when we do."

"I just worry I made the wrong choice."

"No. Don't doubt your choices; just go get out of the house for a while."

"Hey baby girl, we're going to go play with your cousin Aleah for a little while."

"Me pway?" That sparked some life back in her.

"Yes, let's go. Aleah is waiting to play with you at her house." She smiles and toddles off towards the door. This just might be the best medicine for all of us.

Pulling up to Karlie's house we see a small bundle of energy come running out the front door with my sister following behind with a smile as wide as her face.

"My tousin?" She's trying desperately to get out of her car seat so she can run to Aleah.

"Yes but let me get you unbuckled first, silly. Okay, now to play." I smile when she runs as fast as she can up to Aleah. The girls give each other a big hug when they get close enough and at that moment I know without a doubt I did the right thing bringing her here.

"They're going to be best friends for life." Karlie gives me a hug of reassurance.

"I think you're right. I've been doubting my decision to move her here but after seeing that; no more."

"It'll all work out Jonathan; she needed to be home with her family. So did you."

"I know that but Lizzie is her family too."

"Yes but Lizzie was one person. Here she has more than she can count."

"I know, I really do. It's just that I feel so guilty for ripping her away from her life there."

"You're feeling guilty for hurting Lizzie you mean."

"Of course I feel guilty for taking Arianna away from her."

"You didn't take her away from her. You're Arianna's father and if you had known about her all along she wouldn't have been with her aunt to begin with. None of this is your fault big brother, you're simply making the hard decisions in Arianna's best interest."

"When did you get so smart?" I hug my know-it-all little sister and feel so grateful to have her in my life. Grateful to have such great people here to lean on.

"I was thinking about throwing a party, like a baby shower type of thing for you and Arianna."

"A baby shower? She's not exactly a baby anymore."

"You know what I mean. Aaron's wife owns a party planning business and she said she'd love to help. There's a lot of stuff you'll need for Arianna and it'll be a way for everyone to show their support for you. We're all so proud of how you stepped up and took responsibility."

"All of those people want a party or you want a party?"

"It will be a way to get reacquainted with everyone again too."

"I have been gone a long time."

"Yay! That's a yes right?"

"Please don't squeal, you're already hurting my arm from squeezing it."

"I love you big brother!" She wraps her arms around me again.

"What have I done?" I smile and laugh as she scurries inside already making plans via cell phone. Oh boy, this is going to be a huge production with Karlie in charge of it.

25

I wake up alone to an almost eerily silent house. I don't remember the last time I've heard absolutely nothing. Rolling over I look at the clock and see it's almost noon. Wow I slept in more than I have since I was in college. I might be able to get used to this life, after all.

That is, until I walk into the stark white kitchen that shows no sign of human life. No dishes in the sink, nothing on the counters or the island. It's almost like I'm looking at a photo in a magazine. So different than the messy lived-in apartment I came from.

Not being able to look at the cold furnishings anymore I decide to throw myself into work again. I'll be done with Janet's painting in no time at this rate. But as I walk into the makeshift studio I stop dead in my tracks as the canvas I've been working on comes into view. I'm supposed to be doing a piece depicting Central Park at night but what I see is anything but. It's a painting of a familiar man holding his little girl. It's the exact picture that I took of them a day or two after they met. It's actually one of my favorite photos of Arianna; how in the world did I paint this without knowing? Gosh did Tanner see it? Maybe that's why he didn't say much to me last night. That has me wondering now. Did he see it before coming home at midnight? He couldn't have, right? He didn't let me know he was leaving this morning either. I type a short message and hit send.

> *Hi. How has your day been so far?*

No reply. He's usually so quick with an answer.

> *Tanner what's going on? You didn't wake me when you left this morning.*

I text again. Still no reply. Something is definitely up. Maybe I should go to his office and find out why he won't talk to me. I decide that that's exactly what I need to do and head to the closet. I'll need to change into public appropriate clothing; nothing with paint stains, that should be tough.

**

"Aaron. Austin."

"Hey Jonathan. Nice to see you home safely. It's been a while. How are things?" Aaron says and shakes my hand. Austin stands behind waiting for his turn.

"It's good to be back in the states and try this civilian thing."

"Good to have you back. Leah and I always keep the flag up at the nursery." Austin says proudly.

"Well thanks. I can't tell you how good it feels to be home. My bed is a lot smaller than I remember but it's still comfy." We all laugh and it feels so good to do that again.

"So are you sticking around for a while now that you've got your little lady over there?" Aaron asks pointing to Arianna who is elbow deep in the sand bucket.

"Yes I've got to find a real job now. No more vacations to sand covered Hell." I joke but they don't laugh.

"We all know those tours were never vacations for any of you. What you and all the other soldiers do over there is nothing short of amazing." Austin says no longer smiling.

"You know, it's great to hear others say that once in a while."

"You men and women are beyond brave. Without you, we wouldn't have the lives we do. Thank you for your service." Aaron slaps me on the back and walks to where Karlie's sitting in the grass watching the girls play in the sandbox.

"Do you guys know of anyone hiring around town?"

"Leah and I've got it covered at the nursery now that she's back to work. If you'd have come back while she was on maternity leave I would've jumped on it."

"Maybe she would like to stay home with Adalynn. Have you asked her Austin?" Karlie questions.

"I told her she could stay home but you know her; she straps the carrier to her chest and goes about her day."

"Amie's going to be the same way. Nothing will slow that woman down."

"Is there something you need to tell us?" Karlie jumps up and screams.

"Whoa calm down there Jack-in-the-Box. I was meaning the future some time; you know, not now."

Karlie sits down almost pouting while all of us men laugh at the sight.

"We all know where Aleah gets it now." Aaron says and pats Karlie on the head.

"You're the only one of us without any kids, old man. You're going to be too old to have kids in the next year or two." There's the Karlie I know and love.

"She's got you there, man. At least she'll get off my back now that I've got Arianna."

"I don't know how my little brother deals with your smart mouth every day." Aaron jokes and dodges a punch coming his way from

Karlie.

"Why don't you give Jonathan a job, Grandpa?" She says quickly and takes off running for the house as Aaron picks up the garden hose.

"How did you live with her as a child? What am I saying? She was with us out of the 6AB just as much!" Aaron winds the hose back up and lifts his hands up as a sign of surrender.

"It's so good to be home; even with my little sister's sassy mouth!"

"I could get you on one of my crews here if you want to do construction. Do you know what you want to do or what interests you?"

"A job working with my hands sounds good right about now. At least until I figure out what I want to do long term. I can't let mom support me and Arianna forever."

"Well, come by the job site on Parker Road and we'll get you started."

"I really appreciate it, Aaron."

"No problem. We've got so many jobs lined up we'll be booked for years."

"That's a great problem to have."

"No doubt. I'll see you all later. Back to work." Aaron waves and I see Austin pondering something.

"What's up Austin? You look like your head's about to explode."

"We've been wanting to expand the nursery and I was thinking that maybe Aaron should set you up there with a few guys. I know he's been trying to make time for our job for a long time. I think I'm gonna go talk to him right now about it."

"Wherever he wants me to go I'll go."

"Great to have you home. Talk later." And just like that the Blake brothers are gone.

"They sure ran out of here like we had the plague." Karlie says coming back outside.

"Probably all of your sass." I smile at her and she rolls her eyes at me.

"Are you sweet girls ready for some lunch?" She leans down and starts wiping the sand off of both girls then herds them inside. It's amazing to see how natural Karlie is as a mother.

"It's been great getting out of the house and great for her too."

"Does Mom have my room demolished yet?"

"She told you about her plans?"

"It was my idea."

"Ah, that was very nice of you. I appreciate it. Arianna had her own room before and I think it'll be good for her to have one here also."

"Every girl needs her own space, you dummy." I shake my head at the name she's always used since we were kids. Some things never change. I can't keep the smile off my face and hug my little sister tight. I can't say it enough; I really did miss these people and this place. Very much.

26

"Can I help you?" A blonde woman sitting at the front desk says.

"Yes, I'm here to see Tanner. Is he in?" She looks at me strangely.

"I believe he's in a meeting. Can I tell him your name?" she asks before standing.

"Lizzie." I'm trying not to feel inferior here. This is my fiancé's world and they don't even know me or me them.

"I'll go see if he's available. Please have a seat." As I do I see another woman and a small child come off the elevator, wave at the other receptionist and walk the way the blonde went. Clearly everyone knows who she is and she knows where she's going.

A few minutes later the blonde bimbo comes back frowning at me. "He says he's busy at the moment but will meet you at the small café around the corner for lunch."

"In a few or right now?"

"He said as soon as he can get there." She gestures to the elevator meaning full well for me to exit.

"Um well, thank you." I say as nicely as I can choke out. This is all so strange; why wouldn't Tanner come tell me this himself? What a way to make me feel welcome.

I've been sitting at this little outdoor table at the café I was directed to for over an hour. An hour! I don't understand what is going on here and I'm getting more unsure about things with every minute that ticks away.

"Ma'am I've got a message for you." I look to find the waiter handing me a piece of folded up paper.

"Thank you." I unfold the note to find Tanner's handwriting.

Liz,

This meeting is going to last all day. See you at home later. Very sorry.

Tanner

You have got to be kidding me! Now he isn't coming at all? After I drove all the way here through terrible traffic, waited over an hour at the restaurant that I was herded to and now this? Wow I'm beside myself. This is ridiculous!

***

"Mom this room looks great and by the look of things; I would say she loves it too." We both look at Arianna and smile at the sight of her laying on her freshly made bed with the teddy bear I got her, sound asleep.

"Aleah must have worn her out. Karlie said she was out cold too."

"It was so good for both of them. And you."

"Yes me too. I got a job while we were there."

"Really? Do tell."

"Aaron's going to add me to one of his crews. I've got to go by the job site tomorrow to hammer out the details."

"You might as well go now; no need to wait. Arianna's napping and I can stay here with her."

"Well then, okay. I'll go now. He said he'd be at a job site on Parker Road."

"Yes, that's Josh and Missy Logan's; they're having a new house built. You remember Missy don't you? She used to be Missy Vanderbilt."

"Vaguely. I think she was a year behind me in school, right?"

"Yes, her younger brother Marty was in Karlie's class."

"Okay yea. I'll be back as soon as I can." I kiss her cheek and head to Parker Road.

"Hey man. I didn't expect to see you so soon." Aaron says and shakes my hand.

"Mom insisted I come now; so here I am." We both laugh at the thought of doing what Mama tell us to.

"Come on in here and I'll introduce you to my right hand."

I follow him into what looks like the start of the kitchen and find a woman standing there looking over a set of house plans. That doesn't look like the Missy I remember.

"Jonathan this is Monica she's my assistant, secretary and my other wife sometimes." He jokes and the woman hits him in the arm. She's his right hand? I didn't see that one coming.

"Nice to meet you." I smile and am taken aback by her smile. Wow she's beautiful. What in the world is this refined woman doing in Colvin working on a construction site? She walks around the table to shake my hand and I'm stunned to see she's got heels and a skirt on too.

"So you're Karlie's big brother right?"

"Guilty." I mentally shake my head to clear it.

"Monica worked for me when I had the other company in the big city. She moved here to help me start over. She's the best thing we've got around here. Keeps us all on our toes, for sure."

"Well I've got that meeting to get to. Hence the heels and girly clothes. Nice to finally meet the soldier big brother." She smiles and walks out of the room.

"Might want to shut your mouth before flies get in it. Oh and word to the wise, don't let Carter see you looking at her like that."

"Carter her boyfriend?"

"Ha ha he wishes. He's fighting hard to get her to even go on a date with him."

"Got it. She's off-limits. Does she always dress like that on job sites?"

Aaron laughs, "Oh no. She hates dressing like that but she's got a big meeting with the bank this afternoon. She's wanting to buy a house over on 4th St."

"Ah, so she's staying here then."

"Goodness I hope so. She seriously keeps this business going."

"Very nice. Now, where do you want me to start or should I say when?"

"Austin just left a few minutes ago and he had a great idea about me appointing you foreman over at Stampley's and giving you a few guys to get started there."

"Foreman? Man you really don't have to do me any favors because of Karlie. I'm fine being just one of the guys."

"Oh no, it's nothing like that. I know you've got excellent leadership skills and would be perfect for this."

"I'm glad to have work wherever it be."

"Give me a couple of days to get things lined up and I'll let you know when it's all ready. Or heck you know what, since its Thursday how about you just show up Monday. I'll meet you there with all the guys and we'll go from there."

"Sounds good; thanks again Aaron."

"No problem at all. You're actually helping me too. They've been wanting me to get that job started for a year if not more. See you Monday."

***

After I get back home from Tanner's office and that entire debacle, I go straight to my artwork. I set the painting of Arianna and her dad aside and actually get started on Janet's Central Park piece. I should've started this one long before now. I'm looking forward to the distraction.

Before I know it, darkness has fallen outside and I look for my phone to check the time. I'm startled to find Tanner standing in the doorway quietly watching me.

"Tanner, you startled me. How long have you been standing there?"

He smiles a small smile, "Sorry, I didn't want to interrupt your genius."

"How long have you been home?"

"I've been home a couple of hours but only watching you for a bit."

"You've been home that long? Why didn't you let me know?" I hear my voice go too high.

"You didn't hear me come in and I saw that you were engrossed in your work."

"I wouldn't have minded if you'd interrupted me. I'm sorry I didn't hear you. What do you think so far?" I shift the canvas towards him.

"It's amazing. Did you finish the other one you were working on?" I believe I see anger flash across his face but he masks it just as fast. He did see the other one. Uh oh.

"That was just me messing around and getting everything situated."

"Did you paint it from memory?"

"I guess so. I have the photo on my phone though."

"You didn't even realize you were painting them did you?" Now the anger is as clear as day on his face.

"No, not really. I was missing her so much that I guess I subconsciously painted her."

"And him. You miss him too, don't you?" There may be smoke coming from Tanner's ears now.

"Tanner please. Where is this coming from?"

"I came home yesterday around six to find you engrossed again in your work but you were painting him."

"But you didn't get home until almost midnight last night and you told me you would be home before three."

"I know. I was late getting here but when I did I saw the painting. I left again because I was angry when I saw who you were painting. I went back to my office until I couldn't stay awake any longer. I had almost talked myself out of being jealous but you were still painting them when I did come back."

"I'm sorry Tanner. It doesn't mean anything. She's with him now and I think it was my way of accepting it."

"Do you love him?" He finally looks directly at me instead of everywhere but.

"Of course not. He became my friend but nothing more. I said I would marry you didn't I?"

"Yes you said it but you don't act it. I keep telling myself it's because of losing Arianna like that that you've been so distant but then you weren't painting just her. It made me question us even more."

"Is that why you wouldn't see me today? Were you punishing me?" Now I'm the one livid.

"Not exactly. I really did have meetings all day but I couldn't face you yet. When you showed up at my office I still wasn't sure that I wanted to introduce you as my fiancé to everyone when I wasn't 100% positive that you were going to stay my fiancé."

"Are you breaking up with me Tanner? Because if you are this is crappy timing. All of my stuff just got here yesterday!" I yell angrily.

"Of course not. I'm just trying to be honest with you like I wish you would be with me."

"I am being honest with you. I don't know what else you want me to say."

"Nothing I guess. I'm sorry maybe I just overreacted at the sight of the painting. I love you Liz and I can't wait for you to be my wife.

Are you ready to set a date yet?"

"Tanner already? I've had so much happen this week and I'd like to get settled into a new normal before I can even think about planning a wedding." Ok maybe I should cut him a break; this can't be easy for him either.

"I understand. I really do. Your whole world's been shaken up, I just don't want you getting away from me again." He slowly pulls me close and presses his lips to mine.

I pull away and ask, "What do you want for dinner? I can make us something."

"Nothing I want is found in the kitchen." And he kisses me again with more passion this time and I swear there has to be sparks coming from between us. My head is telling me to stop this after what all was just said between us but my body is telling me to forgive and forget. And at this moment my body is winning the battle.

27

A few weeks later I've just finished up a long hard day at Stampley's and am ready to head home when I see a brunette woman walking up the street. At first my heart catches because I could swear it was Lizzie but the woman crosses the street and struts over towards me and I see it isn't Lizzie at all.

"Well hello there handsome. I've been walking by here for weeks hoping you would notice me. Today must be my lucky day." She smiles and I see that she's a beautiful girl but just does nothing for me.

"I'm sorry. I thought you were someone else. Have a nice evening." I climb in my pickup and drive away leaving the pretty woman dumbfounded.

"What is wrong with you man? She was obviously into you and she was gorgeous. You're never going to find anyone as great as Lizzie. That's what the problem is." I groan from frustration. Is this ever going to get easier?

"Jonathan, Arianna learned a new word today. Aleah and Karlie came over to play this afternoon. Arianna tell your Daddy what you want to eat for supper." Mom says lifting Arianna up into her booster seat when I walk in the front door.

"Sketti and cawwots." She beams very proud of herself and a smile spreads on my own face.

"Ah baby that's great! Good job!" I lean down and hug my little girl. After the last few minutes I had before getting here; seeing her makes my heart ache a little less.

"The girls heard Karlie and I talking about the recipe for spaghetti. Glad they pick up on the good things first." She smiles almost guilty.

"What's that look for?"

"Oh Karlie said a word we were really afraid the girls would pick up."

"Why did she say a cuss word? Karlie hardly ever cusses."

"She stubbed her toe on the couch while tickling the girls. And without thinking she said the S word but thankfully recovered before they caught on."

"So you taught them another S word to side track them?" I laugh at the genius tactic.

"Well, I guess we did. Now go wash up for dinner." She dishes up each of our plates while I do as I'm told, once again.

"How was the site today?"

"Good. Really making progress. I think we'll be right on schedule for the early October completion date."

"That will be just in time for Austin and Leah to get the Thanksgiving and Christmas shipments in. That's going to be so nice."

"Yes I believe it will." I say flatly.

"Still not big on the holidays?"

"No. But I guess now I'd better learn to love them." We both look at Arianna.

"She's going to love Christmas this year. And even dressing up for Halloween."

"Yep. So what all did you do today Arianna? Besides learn to say carrots and spaghetti?"

"Mama wuv me?" She asks quietly. Mom and I both suck in a quick breath of surprise.

"Of course she does. Why do you ask?" I get up and go kneel down next to her chair.

"Awea mama wuv her. Where my Mama?" She asks putting her hand on my cheek to ensure my attention.

"She's back in North Carolina. I'm sure she's thinking of you all the time." I look at Mom not really sure where to go from here.

"Your Mama loves you very much Arianna. After your bath tonight you and Grandma will go in your room and call her. Okay?"

"YAY! Me eat all gone."

"Whew that was quick thinking on your part. I wasn't sure what to say or do there."

"I could tell by the fear written all over your face. We all know you miss her too."

"I do. I saw a woman walking down the street right before I came home and for a split second I could have sworn it were Lizzie. Of course it wasn't and when the woman thought I was interested I had to tell her no."

"Why don't you start dating? There are lots of women interested."

"Just don't feel interested in any of them."

"None of them are Lizzie."

"Right again Mother." We both go back to finishing our meal. I can tell Mom's wheels are turning in her head and that can't mean good things for anyone. Especially me.

***

Tanner has been trying to be home more these past couple of weeks but he still has meetings at night which menas I'm left alone in this stark house. I usually stay hidden away in the room I've made my studio but now that all of the client orders have been fulfilled I'm left with time on my hands to conjure up my own projects.

I've painted a few portraits of Arianna always making sure her father isn't included in them. The walls of the house are beginning to show that an artist lives here and not just a businessman. If only Tanner would allow me to warm the place up more than hanging artwork. Definitely doesn't feel like home.

Standing in the living room looking at the expanse of black leather, white marble tables and absolutely no curtains. I can't help but think of what a mess Arianna would make of this place. It's definitely not kid friendly. I'm broken out of my thoughts by the faint sound of my cell phone ringing from the studio. I rush to find it and am so excited to see Ella Mae's face on the screen.

"Hello Ella Mae. How are you? Oh I'm doing good. How's my girl? Oh I would love to. Hi baby girl. How are you? What have you been doing? Oh you did? You like spaghetti now? Oh you and Aleah have been playing every day? How nice. I bet you are enjoying that. Yes I've been painting every day. I have quite a few of you hanging on the walls now. Yes I miss you too sweet girl. I'll come visit you soon. Love you so much. Hugs and kisses. Thank you for letting me talk to her Ella Mae. It was so good to hear her little voice. But hard too. I miss her so much it's excruciating. I'm glad she's doing so well down there though.

She sounds so happy. Oh really? I will see what's going on and maybe I can come. When did you say it was? Okay I'll talk to Tanner. I have to ask, how is Jonathan? Is he doing okay being a single dad? Well I guess he's got all of you though so he's not doing it on his own. That's good to hear. Um, is he dating anyone? Not at all? Interesting. I would have thought he'd have lots of girls lined up once he got back. Well, he will when he's ready I guess. Not that I know but isn't that what most people say? Haha well I will let you go and I'll keep you posted on whether I can come to the party. I'll try my best to make it. What will he think about me coming? Will he be mad? Ok if you think so. I'll talk soon. Thanks again for letting me talk to her. Good bye Ella Mae."

I hang up the phone and feel myself start to fall apart again. It's been a few weeks since Arianna moved with Jonathan to Oklahoma so you'd think things would be getting easier to deal with. But they aren't. I miss her more every day and it's killing me to not be able to see her. I see her everywhere I look even after leaving the apartment.

If I'm honest with myself it's also killing me not being able to see Jonathan too but we won't go there. Tanner gets very upset when that name is mentioned so I've had to refrain from saying it.

We've been fighting a lot more than before about Arianna because he thinks I should be focusing on him, setting a date and planning the wedding so we can start having kids of our own. But I'm not really ready for any of that. Especially the having other kids part. All I want right now is to see Arianna, not replace her. He doesn't see it as replacing though so we butt heads about it constantly.

I can only imagine what he's going to say about us going to Colvin for the party Karlie is throwing for Jonathan and Arianna. I wish I knew how to talk him into going. I would love nothing more than to go and see them again. I mean see her again. See, and I wonder why Tanner is the way he is. Lizzie you're an idiot.

***

"Did she get to talk to Lizzie?" I ask as Mom comes into the living room after bathing and getting Arianna into bed.

"She did. Lizzie was very thankful to get to hear her voice."

"I bet. Did Arianna go to sleep okay?" I have to change the subject. Talking about Lizzie kills me. Thinking about how upset she had to be talking to Arianna and having to say goodbye doesn't make it any easier.

"Have you talked to her at all since the morning we left?"

"Mom. You know I haven't."

"Why not? You feel so strongly about her and we can all see that you miss her. Why don't you reach out to her?"

"Because she's engaged and I highly doubt he wants me talking to her."

"You're just making excuses but whatever you need to tell yourself. I'm going to read for a spell then go to bed. Good night Son I love you. You're hard headed but I love you anyway." She kisses my cheek and goes to her room.

I'm left sitting here in the empty living room thinking about the one woman on the planet that I'm not supposed to be thinking about. What if I did call her? Would she even answer?

I pull out my cell phone and scroll for her name. Once I find it on the list I can't make myself push call. Just call me Jonathan the Coward from now on. I've been to Iraq and many other war stricken places and never been a coward. That is until I fell in love

169

with Elizabeth Kentis.

Holy crap. I am in love with her. Now that makes it even worse.

I scroll through my contacts again until I find Tarley's name and picture.

"Hey man! Long time no talk. How ya been? Work's good actually. Feels good to work with my hands all day. What have you been up to? You should come for a weekend or something. It would be great to have you here and introduce you to everyone. Actually Karlie's throwing some party for me and Arianna this weekend. You should come. Of course I'll pick you up. Let me know the flight details. It will be great to catch up. Awesome see you then. Later."

Tarley is coming to Colvin. This is going to be an amazing weekend. He didn't really sound like himself so it'll do us both good to be around each other again. I've got to keep him away from my sister though. I laugh knowing Aiden and his brigade will do that for me.

Shortly after hanging up with Tarley I decide it's time for bed myself since I've got another couple of full days at Stampley's before the weekend. I'm not so excited about the party but I am about my buddy coming to stay the weekend. I've really missed having him by my side every day.

Maybe having him around will help me get Lizzie out of my head. I can only hope.

28

"Liz? I'm home. Where are you?" I hear Tanner say once he comes in the front door.

"In the studio." Duh, where else would I be?

"Should have known the answer to that question." He comes over and kisses my forehead.

"What are you working on?" He looks at the canvas like he's not sure what's on it.

"It's supposed to be the view from our old balcony. It was the reason Marianna got the apartment that we lived in. She loved the view." I look up at him hoping to see that he likes the painting but instead he's reading an email on his phone.

"It's nice. I have to go return this email." And out the door he went as fast as he blew in.

I need to find the best time to talk to him about the party. Maybe I should make his favorite dinner tonight, chicken alfredo. That way he'll be in a good mood when I broach the subject.

I have cooked an entire meal along with garlic bread and green bean casserole. All of Tanner's favorites.

"Honey, I'm sorry to do this but I have to go back to the office for a little bit. Oh that looks amazing. Keep a plate warm for me and I'll be home later. So sorry." He kisses my forehead again and out the door he goes. Again.

"Seriously? I've been cooking all of this for the past hour and he just leaves? Keep a plate warm? Oh no. He can eat it out of the trash if he wants some." I dish up my own plate, eat it and dump the rest in the garbage can.

"That ought to teach him to never leave for work when I've been slaving away on a meal just for him."

I leave all the dirty dishes, pots and pans all over the kitchen. I don't care what he's going to say when he sees the mess and food in the trash.

I walk to the bedroom, sit on the bed and pull my laptop up onto my knees. Before I realize it I've gone to a travel site and booked a flight for Tanner and myself to Colvin. He's going to flip out but since he left when I wanted to talk to him about it he'll just have to deal with that too.

The next morning Tanner comes into the bedroom and sits next to me gently shaking my arm to wake me.

"Liz you didn't have to throw the food away. That was a waste. And you didn't clean the kitchen. I have spent the past hour cleaning it all up for you. You know I don't like a dirty house."

"I'm sorry I was hurt you left so I lost interest in the meal."

"I'm sorry I left you when you had fixed dinner. George needed a few files form my desk and when I got to the office he and a client were having a drink so I joined them."

"You had a drink with friends while I was here waiting for you with a fully prepared meal sitting on the table?" I sit up now fully away and very upset.

"Oh don't be dramatic. It's not like I went out clubbing."

"Tanner I wanted to talk to you last night about something very important but you stayed at your office having a drink. How nice of you."

"What could you possibly want to talk to me about that couldn't wait until this morning?" He looks at my laptop sitting on the side table. "Why is your laptop in here? I thought we decided that electronics weren't meant for the bedroom?"

"Do I look like a child that needs a lecture for leaving her toys out?"

"No of course not. You're grumpy this morning aren't you?"

"Tanner I booked us flights for Saturday morning to Colvin."

"Colvin? What the heck for? We're not going there."

"Yes we are. They're having a party for Arianna and her dad and we were invited."

"I'm sure it was you who was invited. You're not going either. You might as well get your money back on the tickets. It's not happening. You know how I feel about him Liz."

"I will do no such thing. I'm going to go to that party and see Arianna. And there's nothing you can do about it."

"If you decide to go then when you get back you can move your stuff back out of my house because there won't be an us left." He stands up and walks out the door. Seconds later I hear the front door slam shut and the pictures shake on the walls. He seriously gave me an ultimatum.

"That went well." I frown and throw myself back against the pillows. "What do I do now?"

***

"I really need to go back and get my pickup. I'm tired of driving this clunker that doesn't like to start most of the time." I tell Mom the next morning. I've been trying to get Dad's old pickup started for a half hour and it won't budge.

173

"Just call Maysen, he'll come get it. Take my car today. We don't need to go anywhere. And if we do we'll walk." She hands me her keys.

"I really do need to go back though. I need to get the rest of her stuff and my pickup."

"You'll have time later. No need to go right now. You've got work and Karlie's planned this party for tomorrow. You'll have all kinds of time after to go back to North Carolina."

"Why don't you want me to go back?" Something's fishy here.

"No reason. I'm just stating the obvious. You've got a lot going on. That pickup and a few toys are minor details."

"A brand new pickup sitting in long term parking at an airport in North Carolina is not a minor detail."

"You know what I mean Son. You can go next weekend. Just not important now."

"Whatever. I'll be back later. I'll stop by and see Maysen on the way. Bye."

I pull up to Correli Repair and see Maysen walking out the door towards me.

"Hey man. Your Mom's car acting up again?"

"Oh no, actually it's Dad's old Ford. I've been driving it since I came back but I can't get it to stay running. Think you could bring it in and see what's going on?"

"Sure. I thought I heard you bought a brand new Chevy?"

"Yes but as Mom puts it, it's a minor detail that's sitting in long term parking at the Charlotte airport."

"Ouch. Those babies aren't cheap either. I'll bring your Dad's old pickup here later this morning and look it over. Should know something by end of day."

"Thanks man. Appreciate it. Give me a call if you need anything."

"You're working with the crew at Stampley's right?"

"Yes sir. Which reminds me I'd better grace them with my presence before Aaron fires me." We both laugh and I head to the job site in my Mother's car. How manly.

"Hey glad you could finally make it. The pickup again?" Aaron says as I walk up to the crowd of guys at Stampley's.

"Yes. Maysen's going to go get it this morning. I've got to go get my new one in Charlotte."

"He'll take care of you. He's a whiz with cars."

"I'm stuck with Mom's car to take to Tulsa tonight too."

"Hot date?" Austin asks grinning from ear to ear.

"Yea right. If you want to call my old Army buddy Tarley hot." I laugh at the thought.

"Oh that's right. Karlie told us your buddy was coming to town this weekend for the party. You can always take my pickup if you'd feel better about it." Austin says motioning towards his pickup that has a big Stampley's sticker on the side.

"I think I'll pass."

"Hey Leah thinks it's best to advertise everywhere we go. It killed me putting that on the new ride though."

"You're whipped enough to do it." Aaron jokes.

"You're one to be talking. Where is your pickup right now?" Austin asks smiling like a kid with a secret.

"Shut up. She wanted to give me a ride today. What's wrong with that?" Aaron says getting a little red in the face.

"Aaron Blake blushes?" Austin snorts and receives a big slug from Aaron.

"I love my wife. What can I say?"

"And I love mine."

"Ok guys you're even. You're both sappy and in love while some of us here can't even get a date!" I spit out not realizing what I had just said until all of them look at me.

"Can't get a date? Heck you can't narrow them down. Oh wait, you turn them all down." Aaron says and slaps me on the back.

"How do you all know about those?"

"It's Colvin man. Nothing is secret here." Austin says and smiles before returning inside the nursery.

"Oh boy. That's something I haven't missed."

"Maybe you should call the one you're so hung up on?"

"Why Aaron have you been talking to my little sister?"

"No. Amie talked to her and talked to me about it when she heard you were working for us."

"The rumor mill in full swing. Awesome." I walk away to get the guys started and get my day started before anyone else wants to talk about my love life. Or lack there of.

29

"Zandra I really don't know what to do. Do I go and deal with Tanner when I get back or do I stay, patch things up with him and miss the party?"

"Girl I came over here to help you pack for Colvin. Not to go back and forth with what you should and shouldn't do."

"You came over here to be my friend."

"Yes I did. But I also think you're being a fool for even thinking about canceling your trip. You and Tanner happened at the wrong time. You're not meant to be together. You never have been."

"Wow you put it right out there."

"Do you want me to sugar coat it for you? No, you know that wouldn't help you any. Go get your luggage and we're going to find the most amazing outfits for your trip."

"You really want me to go don't you?"

"I don't really care about the trip, I just want you to lose the current loser boyfriend."

"He's not a loser. He's very successful and loves me."

"Maybe so but he's not the one you love, now is he?" She asks looking directly at me waiting on my answer but already knowing what it is.

"No."

"See, now say it and it'll be all better."

"Say what exactly?"

"You love Jonathan and you know it."

"Ugh you're right. I love Jonathan and I think I have since I first heard his voice over the phone."

"Then that's the answer to all your problems. You're going to Oklahoma to find your man." She starts throwing clothes out of my closet from all directions.

"But what do I do about all of my stuff? I just got it all here and I gave up my apartment."

"You can move it all into mine. Actually I'll call the movers in a few minutes and get them here today before you leave."

"You're moving me out today?"

"Why wait? Are you really going to be able to stay in this house with Tanner tonight after he gets home?"

"No probably not."

"Then it's settled. I'll get your stuff moved and when you come back, if you come back, you'll never have to come back to this cold house."

"Wow. My life continues to flip upside down. That's about all it's done since Marianna got sick. Just when I think things are going to settle down, something else happens."

"Well, you get your art room packed up. That's the only place I know you'll be picky about when the movers come. I'll get you packed for your trip."

"Deal. I hate packing for a trip anyway."

"And I'll make sure you've got all the sexy outfits that will snag you a sexy soldier while you're there." She screeches out and smiles before going back to throwing clothes everywhere.

I'm moving out of Tanner's house. For real. I'll be out before he comes home from work. What will he think when he comes in and finds no trace of me? I'm not sure it'll bother him.

***

"Man it is so good to see you!" Tarley and I hug when he comes into view in the airport terminal.

"Jonathan the tough guy missed me? You're turning into a total sap aren't you?" He pretends to wipe a tear from his eye.

"I can't help it. Arianna changed me."

"That's evident. I'm really happy for you man. You deserve to be happy after all the crap we've been through over the years." He looks almost lost. The smile didn't make it to his eyes.

"Man what's been up with you? I haven't really heard from you since we got back."

"I didn't wanna bother you since you had such deep stuff to deal with."

"It would have been nice to hear from you too though."

"I'm here now man let's enjoy it. I'm ready to see that hot sister of yours." He smiles wide and I just shake my head. He's going to get a big shock when he sees my sister's husband and his brothers.

"You're asking for trouble."

"Let's get out of this airport and get somewhere I can have a beer."

"That I can do. This way."

An hour or so later we've made our way back to Colvin and are getting ready to enter into Mom's house where it looks to be the happening place tonight. There are pickups parked everywhere and you can hear laughter from inside the house.

"There always this many people around?" He asks almost nervously. That's a strange way to perceive the toughest man I've ever met. I have to be seeing things wrong.

"No. I think they're here to see you."

"All of them?"

"It's just my family and some of my sister's in laws. We're all one big family here."

"How big are we talking?" He really looks scared now.

"Hey man what's up? Are you okay?"

"Of course I'm okay. What kind of question is that?"

"You've been a little off since I picked you up. If you don't want to meet all of them tonight you don't have to. We can wait until tomorrow at the party."

"It's no sweat. Let's go." He climbs out of the car and grabs his bag from the trunk. I swear there is something off about him. He's obviously not going to tell me though. I get out of the car and lead the way inside the crowded house.

"Guys. And ladies. This is my buddy Tarley. Without him I wouldn't be standing in front of you all tonight. He and I went through Hell together so many times and because of each other we always made it back." I slap him on the back and motion for him to say hi.

"Hi everyone. It's really not as big of a deal as he makes it sound. He's the tough one, not me." He looks down at the ground clearly uncomfortable with the spotlight.

"Well, this is my little sister Karlie whom you've seen pictures of over the years, her husband Aiden and little girl Aleah. Aiden's older brothers Aaron, Austin and little sister Audrey. Aaron's wife is Amie over there. Austin's wife is Leah over there holding the little girl named Adalynn. The last guy there would be Audrey's husband Maysen holding their son, Abbott. The whole bunch's mother and father Amelia and AJ Blake. Lastly the two women I'm currently shacking up with, my mother Ella Mae and my little girl Arianna."

"Nice to meet you all. I've heard so much about all of you over the years it's almost like I've met you before."

"We have also heard a lot about you. Thank you for keeping my son alive and being there for him when he needed someone the most. You'll forever be a part of this family. Can I give you a hug Tarley?" Mom asks waiting for confirmation. Tarley finally nods and Mom wraps him up in her arms. If I didn't know better I would think he had a few tears fall while Mom was suffocating him.

"Okay let's get all of these big guys fed." Mom ushers the group to the dining room where the biggest feast since Thanksgiving has been laid out for us.

"Wow ma'am you didn't have to go to all of this trouble just for me." Tarley says hesitant to join the group.

"You're a special young man and we are very proud to finally meet you. Now sit and dig in!" He too does as Mom tells him. She's so bossy. I smile knowing that will never change.

30

"That's all of it girl. The movers are going to drop your stuff off at my place in a bit so we'd better get over there."

"Yep. Give me a minute to leave Tanner a note."

"Ok, he's going to have quite the shock tonight isn't he?" She smiles big clearly enjoying this a little too much.

"I'm afraid so." I turn and walk into Tanner's home office in search of a pen and something to write on. I pull his desk chair out and sit down. Looking around the large office space I'm not surprised to see that it's minimally decorated like the rest of the house. This man loves his bland décor. Opening the middle desk drawer I'm not surprised to see the contents are all black and white; neatly lined up in rows.

Dear Tanner,

I'm sorry things happened the way they did with us. Please know you are an amazing man; just not the one for me. We tried to force things to work again and they just couldn't.

Thank you for being there for me this past couple of weeks when things were so hard. I know you did your best to do what was needed and I'm very sorry you even had to deal with my drama.

You will make the right woman very happy one day and I pray you find her soon. You've got a lot of love to give and will make a wonderful husband and father.

Take care and know I will forever be grateful for the time I got to spend with you.

Liz

I take off Tanner's diamond ring and look at it one last time. It truly is an amazing ring but not for me. It can't be mine and neither can Tanner. We just don't fit. I lay the ring down on top of the letter. I feel so guilty and terrible for doing things this way but I know we would only be rehashing the same thing over and over if we did it in person.

"Okay, let's go. It's time. Past time actually." And we walk out of Tanner's house. I turn one last time to look at the stark décor realizing that this was never my home and I was never going to feel at home in it.

Especially not when my heart was in Oklahoma.

***

"Morning sunshine. How'd you sleep?" I ask Tarley the next morning when he comes out of the spare bedroom at almost ten o'clock.

"Wow it's ten? I haven't slept this late in ages. What did you drug me with last night Mrs. Doone?" He jokes and sits next to me on a barstool.

"Please call me Ella Mae. You slept well I take it?" Smiling she slides a plate of breakfast up to Tarley.

"Wow and a home cooked breakfast? I could get used to this lifestyle. No wonder you came home." He slaps me on the back and digs in.

"Is there anything you ladies need help with this morning before the party? She's gone over board hasn't she?" I ask not really wanting to hear the answer to that question.

"I think we have it handled. If you'll keep track of Arianna and come out to the AK when Karlie tells you to then we'll be good."

"I can do that. I'll show Tarley around town and maybe take Arianna to the park for a bit."

"Is there that much to see that I didn't see on the way in? This place is so small." Tarley questions.

"Man, you only saw parts of it and it was dark. Just wait."

"Are there women to be seen too?"

"You haven't changed a bit." I laugh and head to Arianna's room shaking my head.

"Hey baby girl. Are you ready to get dressed? How about we take Tarley around town and then to the park?"

"Pway park?" She jumps up and down squealing. She got that from my sister I'm afraid.

"Yes you can play at the park. Now, let's get you dressed. Tarley's eating his breakfast right now." I proceed to help a squirming toddler put on her clothes. Thankfully my mother helps to set them out every day so that she matches. I'm not sure I would know what goes together or care. Poor kid would probably look homeless if it were left up to me.

"Ready when you are man. Hey pretty little lady. You're not bad at this Dad thing by the way." We turn to see Tarley leaning against the door jamb.

"Thanks. My mom and sister have been such a big help. I'm learning but it's a lot of work. I don't know how Lizzie did it all by herself for so long."

"Ah, the hot aunt. Are you still talking to her?"

"Um no. She was so upset man when we left and I can't make myself call her. Not sure I can hear the hurt in her voice."

"You've turned into a mushy little coward huh?" He laughs.

"Not funny. It's ridiculous because I make my mother call her anytime Arianna wants to talk to her." I say shaking my head and picking up Arianna.

"You really fell for her didn't you?" He looks at me with a shocked expression on his face.

"Well duh. If you saw her you'd understand."

"Oh I remember trying to get you to let me go with you. You told me she was off limits. But not to you obviously." He scowls.

"Oh she's still off limits. Even to me. She's engaged."

"What? When and who?"

"Some ex of hers that came back in the picture not long after I met her."

"Wow. Is that the reason you suddenly came back here? I wasn't sure you were going to leave North Carolina."

"You know, that's probably a big reason. I tried telling myself I needed to get Arianna here with the support of my family and everything but I think not being able to have Lizzie was what made the decision clear."

"Wow. I don't know what else to say but wow."

"Let's go. No more talk about women or anything deep. I'm barely holding onto my man card as it is." I carry Arianna to Mom's car determined to keep Lizzie off my mind today.

31

"Flight 234 to Tulsa now boarding." I hear over the loud speakers in the Charlotte airport the next morning. I'm really doing this. I'm going to Colvin, Oklahoma to see Arianna. And Jonathan.

My stomach flip flops when I think of seeing him again. Being close enough to see his dark eyes and feel his lips on mine.

Whoa. Snap out of it Lizzie. You don't even know if he wants you the same way you do him. He could have been being nice and now has a great girlfriend there. Oh goodness that will be awful if he does. I'm not sure I could see him with another woman. Let alone see the other woman touching him. And Arianna being around her? Ella Mae says he isn't dating so hush.

Oh Heavens maybe I shouldn't be doing this. What if he's not happy to see me? What if he's angry that I came without running it by him first?

"Last call for Flight 234 to Tulsa." Oh crap what do I do?

"It's now or never Lizzie. You have to take this chance. Even if he doesn't want to see you, Arianna will and that's got to be the only thing I'm focusing on right now."

"Hello ma'am can I see your ticket please? Please follow the crowd and find your seat. We will be taking off soon. Thank you for flying with us." I smile and feel the butterflies in my stomach again. Oh boy this is going to be a long flight.

Marianna please let me know I'm doing the right thing. Is this what you want?

If only she were here to tell me the answer.

I walk down the plane's aisle looking for seat 14A but when I get there it's not empty. There's a woman and her little baby is laying in my seat. What am I supposed to do now? Kick the little bundle of joy out of my seat?

I raise my hand and get the flight attendant's attention.

"Excuse me but are there any other seats available? I think she needs my seat more than I do." I motion to the new mother and smile. The flight attendant does the same and lifts a finger saying just a minute.

When she comes back she smiles and says, "Follow me."

We walk back to the front of the plane where first class passengers are and I'm very confused. Surely they aren't kicking me off the whole flight for asking about another seat! There's no way I could afford an upgrade to first class.

"Um I can't afford a seat up here ma'am. Isn't there anything left in coach?"

"No ma'am. This is your new seat. Please make yourself comfortable."

"But I can't afford this seat. There's got to be somewhere else."

"I'm afraid not but the airline will take care of the upgrade fee."

"You're kidding right? They don't just upgrade for free."

"What you did back there for that young mother was selfless. There needs to be more people like you in the world."

"I just didn't want her to have to move the baby. It's nothing really."

"To her it is. Please make yourself comfortable. Have a great flight."

Wow. Just wow. I remember what it's like having a new baby and doing it all alone. I never flew with Arianna but I did try to go shopping once in a while. Just going to the grocery store was a trek.

"First class huh? Ok Marianna I get the picture. I'm doing the right thing. Point taken." I smile pleased with her answer.

***

"So that's all of it? That took like five minutes Jonathan." Tarley jokes after I've finished my tour of Colvin.

"It's a great place though. Maybe you should stay longer than tomorrow." I pull the car up to the park and Arianna starts to freak out in the back seat. "Alright sweetheart you'll get out in a second."

"You know, I've been thinking about maybe doing that. Is there somewhere I could stay for a bit? I don't really want to impose on your Mom."

"There's always room for you at Mom's." I say as I unbuckle Arianna's squirming body from her car seat.

"I couldn't though. You guys have your hands full with her."

"I don't have to baby sit you do I?"

"Well no but she really wouldn't want to have another person living in her house would she?"

"Are you going to live there forever or just until you figure your life out?"

"Temporary. I'll need a job though Mr. Know-it-all. How you gonna handle that one?"

"I can talk to Aaron about hiring you at Double B or there's always ranch work at the AK or 6AB."

"The what or the what? Speak non-Colvin lingo please."

"The AK is the ranch my sister and Aiden have while the 6AB is the one that his parents have."

"And they would hire an old washed up soldier like me?"

"They hire strong men to do the hard work out there. If you want we can talk to them about it today at the party."

"You sure they would want another person working at either of them?"

"You know I'm not sure if AJ ever replaced my Dad after he passed away. He was the foreman on the 6AB as long as I can remember. Maybe that's something you would be good at."

"Hmmm if you think they'd be interested in having me work for them I'll sure talk to them with you."

"Catch me at the party and we'll do it. This just might be what you've been looking for too buddy."

"Who says I'm looking for something?"

"Just know you well enough to know you're not yourself."

"I was trying to hide it from you. Obviously I didn't do a very good job of it."

"Why hide it? We've always been there for each other. No different now that we're out of the service."

"You've got so much going on I didn't want to bother you."

"You are my best friend man. You'd never be a bother."

"Well, the PTSD hit me pretty hard. Did you not have any of it?"

"No, I didn't have any that I knew of. I'm sorry I didn't know you did. You saw a lot more than I did on the front lines."

"You were there too; don't downplay it."

"Are you doing better with the nightmares then?"

"I haven't been but last night I didn't have one for the first time since I got out."

"Really? Maybe being around people who care helped then?"

"I don't know what it was but it was awesome to get that much rest. I feel like a new man today."

"That's great to hear man. Maybe you're meant to be here too. I know I am." I look over at Arianna climbing on the merry go round.

"She's a sweet little lady. You're lucky to have her."

"Yes I am. One day you'll find someone and have one of her too."

"One step at a time man, one step at a time."

"Deal."

32

"We're going to begin our decent into Tulsa. Welcome to Oklahoma. The weather looks sunny and beautiful. Thank you for flying with us today. Good day."

We're here. Seriously already? I've got to go get my rental car and head the hour to Colvin. At least I think it's an hour. The website I got the directions off of said it was about an hour. I wonder if I should call Ella Mae and let her at least know that I'm coming. As soon as we land and I get my rental car I'll do just that. I think I'd feel better knowing someone was going to be okay with me just showing up out of the blue. Well, not out of the blue I was invited. But not by Jonathan. I'm so nervous to see how he reacts to my arrival. Will be he happy or upset? We shall see because it's time to get off the plane. I stand grabbing my bags that I had with me and get ushered toward the open door. I follow the other passengers to search for the sign that says rental cars. The lady said it was easy to find when I called and made the reservation this morning. Aha there it is.

"Hi I have a reservation under Kentis. I called this morning from Charlotte."

"Yes, Elizabeth Kentis. Is that correct ma'am?"

"Yes. Thank you."

After doing all the necessary paperwork I'm settled into the little car I was given. It's a little shoe box for sure; and Marianna thought my midsize car was small. Hmph.

I pull out my cell phone and hit call on Ella Mae's contact.

"Hi Ella Mae, how are you?"

"Well Lizzie please tell me you're calling to say you're here in

Oklahoma for the party."

"Actually I just landed in Tulsa and got my rental car."

"Oh that is so great to hear! Is Tanner with you too?" I can hear a bit of hesitation in her voice.

"Nope. Just little ol' me."

"Well we can't wait to see you and Arianna is going to be beside herself to see you."

"I can't wait to see her either."

"It's about an hour from the airport to Colvin so you'll be here soon enough."

"The directions I printed off the internet said it was about an hour. I'll let you know when I get to town."

"You be careful and go straight to my house when you get there. Jonathan and Arianna should still be there. I might not be but you'll need somewhere to stay tonight."

"Oh no I rented a room at the Colvin B&B. So I'll go there first and change."

"Ok, that will be fine too. I'll make sure Jonathan doesn't leave the house and head to the AK until after you've arrived. You'll get lost trying to get out here all by yourself."

"It's no bother I can just get directions to the party too."

"It's no bother at all. Just go to my house. The address I gave you and Arianna will be there so excited to see you. That way you won't have your homecoming in front of the whole town."

"The whole town?"

"Oh yes I believe everyone is coming to the party."

"Oh boy then I guess it would be best to do it at your house. Does he know I'm coming?"

"He has no clue. Neither does Arianna. I will warn you that his Army friend Tarley is also at the house."

"Oh maybe I should wait until after the party then to stop by?"

"No need. It'll all work out dear, I promise. See you when you get to the party later on. Drive safe."

"I will. Goodbye." I don't feel good about any of this. She doesn't seem to think he'll be upset but what if he is? He may think I'm butting into his life instead of keeping my distance from Arianna.

"What are you talking about? You haven't seen her in weeks. You have every right to see her. He can get over it. His mother invited you anyway."

I put the car in drive and hit the accelerator. Ready or not Jonathan here I come.

***

"Jonathan we have a little surprise for you that isn't going to be ready for about an hour or so. Don't leave the house until I say it's ok. Do you understand me?"

"Yes Mother. What other surprise do you two have in store? This humongous party is enough, nothing else is needed."

"Oh trust me you'll be so happy with this surprise you'll forget all about the party."

Oh wonderful. I'm not so sure I'll be as enthused about their surprise as they are.

"Well, let's get you ready for the party missy. You can hit the shower first if you want man." I say to Tarley as I take Arianna into her bedroom to start the song and dance of getting her clothes changed.

"Alright. Did your Mom say something about a surprise? Isn't the whole town being at a party for you surprise enough?"

"Welcome to my world." I groan and return my attention back to the toddler that won't keep her attention on one thing longer than a second.

"Hey, we have to do the shirt first. Grandma has some sweater contraption that goes over the shirt." Why do baby clothes have to be so complicated. I put a shirt over my head and pull jeans up. Done. This takes thirty minutes just to get her undressed and redressed.

"Dramma? Awea?"

"Yes, once you're dressed we'll go see Grandma and Aleah. You can play with her at her house again. Okay?"

"Yea."

"But you have to help Dada get your clothes changed. You're making it more difficult every time you sit down." Laughing I try to get her standing again.

33

"You're in room 3B. It's on the north side of the hallway just up those stairs. Welcome to Colvin. Hope you enjoy your time here."

"Thank you." I take the room key from the older man and start to walk up the stairs. This is really a beautiful place. I'm so glad I decided to do the B&B instead of the regular motel. I've always wanted to stay in a B&B so now's my chance. Wish I weren't alone but I guess it's better than never.

Opening the door to 3B and I'm first comforted by the smell of lavender and then the view out the window is spectacular. There's a lush garden out there that is calling my name. I set my things down quickly and rush to find the back door.

Once outside I feel the stress start to ease out of my body while I'm thinking about where I would like to set up my easel. This garden would make the best painting inspiration. There's so many different ideas running through my head that I'm not sure I'll be ready to go back to North Carolina tomorrow. This place could start me on a whole new collection of paintings for a new gallery show. I'll have to call Freddie back in Charlotte when I've got the first piece done. He'll want the exclusive on these. Smiling I realize that I feel good being here. I was afraid being in Colvin would be stressful or scary. This is far from.

That is because you're hiding in a garden instead of walking up to a house that is the home of the man you love. And the little girl whom has become your own little girl. Enough hiding out. I need to see Arianna.

I walk around the side of the building towards my car. It's go time. I send Zandra a quick text.

At B&B. Going to their house. Eeek keep fingers crossed.

I don't have to wait long for her reply.

You got this girl! Hugs!

If only I felt that confident about it. I put the car in drive and start down the streets where the directions tell me to go while my heart is racing. My stomach is in knots and I'm not sure if this is what I should be doing but it's a little late now.

I stop at the curb of a large blue house that has pretty white flowers and shutters to match. This is the type of house I've always wanted to live in and raise my own family. This is the house that Jonathan was raised in. And now he's raising his daughter in it. That makes me smile.

Before I know what I'm doing I've reached the front door and see the doorbell. I try to get my hand to touch it but I'm a little scared. Hesitation is all I can feel at the moment. A slight panic hits and I'm ready to turn around when I hear a small voice inside laughing. She's actually screaming and laughing. Sounds like she's being tickled or chased around the room.

That's all it took to make my finger reach the doorbell and push it. I can vaguely here it ring inside and the little voice squeals that someone is at the door. The footsteps are getting closer and closer to the other side of this door. Then it opens.

The most amazing man I've ever seen is standing there looking at me as if he's seen a ghost. No smile but no frown. That can't be bad, can it?

"Hi." That's all you can get out? You've been dreaming of seeing this man again and you can only say one word?

"Lizzie? Is it really you?" He smiles now. Whew that helps.

"Yes. Your mom invited me for your party. Hope it's okay that I came." I stand outside still wringing my hands together afraid of his answer.

"Of course it's okay that you came. Arianna is going to be so happy to see you."

"Where is she? I've missed her so much."

"Oh where are my manners? Come on in. Do you have bags I can help with?" He opens the door wider and steps aside so I can walk through.

"No, I've already checked into my room at the B&B."

"Oh so you're staying the night?"

"Yes, my flight leaves tomorrow afternoon."

"Did you come alone?" He say looking around out the front door.

"Yes Jonathan. Tanner isn't here."

"That's not really what I meant but okay."

"It's not?"

"Well maybe. I'm just surprised you're here. My Mom knew you were coming didn't she?"

"Yes, I talked to her before I left the Tulsa airport."

"That's the surprise I couldn't leave the house because of."

"What?"

"She told me I couldn't leave the house until she said because there was a surprise for me. It must have been you coming here."

"She told me to make sure I came here instead of the party."

"She's a sly one isn't she?" He says smiling and yells out. "Arianna, someone's here to see you."

"Awea? Dramma?" She comes running from another room down the hall but stops as soon as she sees me.

"Hi baby girl." I kneel down hoping she'll come the rest of the way.

"My mama? Dada my mama?" She looks up at Jonathan almost confused.

"Yes, she came to see you." That makes her smile and then she runs full speed into my open arms.

"Mama mama mama mama." It feels like the world has been set right once she's in my arms. My heart is so full which makes tears start to fall from my eyes.

"I have missed you so much Arianna. I love you so very much." I hold her tight not wanting to ever let her go again.

"Wuv Mama." She is holding onto me just as tight. I look up at Jonathan and if I didn't know better I would think he's also tearing up.

"Do you want anything to drink? Eat?" He finally asks shakily.

"No, I'm good. I'm perfect now actually." I look back at Arianna and see she's not letting go either.

"Hey man you about ready to go?" I hear a strange male voice from down the hall. A large man comes into view but when he sees me he stops too. That seems to be the reaction everyone has to seeing me today.

"Um Tarley, this is Lizzie. She came for the party."

"Your Mom's surprise I take it?" The big man smiles and slaps Jonathan on the back.

"I would assume so." Jonathan smiles that smile that makes me go weak in the knees. Good thing I'm already on them or I'd probably fall on my face.

"Good to meet you Lizzie. I've heard a lot about you." He walks to me and extends his very large hand towards me.

I extricate one hand free from Arianna's grasp and shake his hand.

"Nice to meet you as well. I didn't mean to interrupt your reunion. Ella Mae had asked me a couple of days ago to come but I wasn't sure I was coming until yesterday." I stand up but keep Arianna close in my arms.

"Dada my mama. My mama." She kisses my cheek and I feel tears starting to well up in my eyes again.

"I think she missed you a little bit." He smiles at me before getting his cell phone out of his back pocket and calling someone. I would imagine his Mom.

"Hey Mom. You're pretty sneaky aren't you? Yes, she's here. Thank you for inviting her. Arianna is so happy. Yep, we'll see you in a few. Alright, love you."

"How about I take Arianna out back to play for a few minutes and let you two talk before we head to the shin dig." Tarley steps up and asks.

"Arianna will you go outside and play with Tarley while your Daddy and I talk for a minute?" I ask her.

"Mama stay?" She asks wanting reassurance that I'll be here when she gets back.

"Yes, I'm going to the party with you. Is that okay?"

"Pway?" She leans towards Tarley's open arms.

"Let's go play a bit." He takes an excited but hesitant little girl outside leaving Jonathan and I alone.

34

I'm not sure if Tarley's act of kindness was a good thing or not. I don't know what to say to Lizzie. Heck I'm still in shock that she's here. I've been wishing she were here all along and now that she is I'm not real sure what to do.

"So, you're not mad that I'm here?"

"Of course not. I'm actually happy to see you."

"You are? Really? I was afraid you'd be upset that I just showed up."

"Why would I be upset? I've been afraid you were upset with me."

"Why would I be mad at you?"

"Because I haven't called you since we left."

"Your Mom has called me. It's fine."

"I have to confess that I've been a total coward when it came to calling you. I couldn't hear the hurt in your voice."

"The hurt?" She questions. I'm not making this very easy to follow.

"I know me taking Arianna was hard on you and hurt you."

"Well yes but I also knew it was what was best for her."

"Maybe but I still couldn't make myself call you. Mom did it for me every time."

"Oh really? I thought you were just busy."

"No. Cowardly lion." There's that laugh I've only heard lately in my dreams.

"I'm sorry you were feeling that way. You seemed so eager to get her here and I thought you just didn't want to be around me anymore."

"I didn't want to…. Oh boy. I'm really going to do this aren't I?"

"Do what? I'm not following again." She really is confused now.

"I didn't want to see you with Tanner anymore."

"What? Why would that bother you?"

"Because I really liked being around you. And I fell in love with you along the way." Oh my goodness there it is. All laid out on the line.

"Did I just hear you right? I don't think I did." She steps back and that worries me. I think I just scared her away.

"I said I fell in love with you." There. Can't get much clearer than that.

She's just standing there staring at me; clearly speechless.

"It's okay you don't have to say anything. We really do need to get to the party." I turn to walk to the back door so I can call Tarley back in.

Before I can get there she says something that I never thought I would hear come out of her beautiful mouth.

"I love you too Jonathan." She's smiling and wringing her hands again.

I walk to her and take those hands in mine and pull her against me. She wraps her arms around my waist and I hold her as tight as I can possibly get her. I have to be dreaming.

"Lizzie I've wanted to hear that for several weeks." I kiss the top of her head and she sighs into my chest.

"I broke up with Tanner. I told him he just wasn't the one for me."

"You did? Ouch."

"Well, there's a lot more to that story. I'll tell you later okay?"

"Yes, I want to hear it all. But right now we really need to head to my sister's." We both walk to the back door and motion for Tarley to come back inside.

He smiles when he sees that Lizzie is in my arms and points to us for Arianna to see. She beams when realization hits her that we are hugging each other.

"Mama Daddy!" She runs to us and I pick her up not willing to let Lizzie go either.

"Yes, we're both here baby girl. Are you ready to go to Aleah's and party the afternoon away?" I ask her knowing she's been dying to go all day.

"Mama go too?" She questions.

"Yes, I'm going too. Is that what you're wearing out there?" She raises an eyebrow to me when she inspects the clothing Arianna had on.

"My Mother picked it out."

"You've got the skirt on backwards and the vest is inside out. I'll go help her get situated. Where is your room sweet girl?" Arianna takes Lizzie by the hand and directs her to her bedroom. I smile at the sight of Lizzie being here with me and Arianna. Finally.

"That just happened." Tarley says breaking me out of my day dream.

"That did. I'm actually not sure that I'm awake."

"Let me help you with that." And he slugs me in the stomach.

"Ouch! I didn't mean for you to assault me!" We both laugh.

"Are you happy now? She really is hot. If you don't want her I'll gladly take her off your hands." He wiggles his eyebrows at me and I slug him back.

"Absolutely not. She's not going anywhere with anyone but me ever again." I smile meaning every single word.

***

He loves me? That's something I wasn't sure I would ever hear. I have to be dreaming. But the look on Arianna's face when she saw us embracing each other was priceless.

"We really need to get your clothes on right if we're going out in public. Your Daddy doesn't really know how to dress a little girl does he?" I tickle her little tummy making her giggle.

"What's all the giggling in here? You laughing at my expertise in dressing her?" Jonathan says from the doorway. Seeing him standing there smiling at me makes my mouth go dry. Does this man really love little old me?

"You aren't the best at dressing a little girl. That's obvious."

"Good thing we've got you then." He says as he kneels in front of us; kissing each of us on the forehead.

"Yes so she isn't embarrassed at the party. I hear the paparazzi are swarming the place today." I smile only joking.

"Good grief I hope not."

"I was joking."

"Well, Austin's wife is an ex famous model and had a major debacle with her ex-husband. That's a story for later too."

"Wow. Now who is Austin? I thought you only had a sister and her husband's name was Aiden." I'm thoroughly confused.

"You're right. Austin is Aiden's older brother. Well, one of them."

"Good grief how many of them are there?"

"Three boys and the baby is a girl. You'll meet them all today and their families."

"Wow. No wonder you wanted to get back here. Sounds like there's a lot of family support to go around. Especially coming from someone who has no family left." I shake my head and frown.

"Is it going to bother you to be around all of this family today?"

"Of course not. I love seeing happy families. One day I hope to have my own." I'm not sure why I'm blushing but I think I am.

"I kinda already thought you did." He says and pulls me up from the floor. Once he does he wraps his arms around my waist giving me the most passionate kiss I've ever experienced in my life.

"Get a room you two. Geez there are little eyes around too." We break the kiss and look at the doorway where an uncomfortable Tarley is standing.

"Oh get over it. That's going to happen a lot. A lot a lot." Jonathan says and picks up Arianna. "Your clothes look a lot better now."

"It's amazing what it does when they're on properly." I say and smile.

"Can we get this show on the road? I'm sure your Mother is chomping at the bit to know how your little arranged reunion went. And I would honestly like to get out of the way of all this sexual tension." He laughs and walks to the door shaking his head.

"You're just jealous." Jonathan says and puts his hand on the small of my back as we walk to the car.

"Where's your new pickup?" I ask looking around wondering where it is.

"It's still in long term parking at the Charlotte airport." Jonathan frowns. "Now I know why my Mother insisted I wait to go get it."

"Why?" Tarley and I say at the same time.

"Because she knew you were coming and didn't want me to miss seeing you." He beams at me while putting the car in reverse. "So for now, I drive Dad's old beat up pickup and Mom's car."

"His Mom's grandma car." Tarley laughs getting a glare from Jonathan.

"The pickup is in Maysen's shop right now getting fixed." He spits out irritated.

"We better get to the party before every starts to think you flew the coop." Tarley says and laughs.

"You're really getting on my nerves man." Jonathan slugs Tarley in the arm. "Good to have you back."

35

"Jonathan I wasn't sure you were ever going to get here." Karlie shouts over the noise as we enter the house. She looks at Lizzie in question.

I put my arm around Lizzie's waist and pull her close for the introduction.

"Karlie, this is Lizzie. Lizzie, this is my pain in the butt little sister." The women smile and say pleasantries to each other. That is until my sister pulls Lizzie in for a big hug.

"I'm a hugger. I'm so glad to finally meet you. I was afraid you'd turn down our invitation." She looks shyly at me.

"So you were in on the surprise too?" I can't help but smile. This is one surprise I will forever be happy about.

"Thank you for the invitation. I'm glad to be here and it was great to finally meet you. Now that I see you in person I can clearly see that Arianna does look just like you." She smiles widely at my sister.

"She's such a great little girl. You did such a good job with her."

"She was easy." Lizzie says very uncomfortable with the praise from Karlie.

"Well, I need to introduce her to everyone. Thanks again for the party and my surprise." I give Karlie a hug and kiss her forehead.

"I'm so glad you were able to join us Lizzie. We should talk later." And Karlie walks away smiling like a kid on Christmas.

"She's proud of herself now." I say tightening the arm I have around her waist still.

"This looks like a great party. She should be proud of it." Lizzie says unaware of what my true meaning is.

"She's proud that she got you here with me. She knew how I felt about you and now you're here with me. And I'm so happy." I kiss Lizzie lightly on the lips drawing awes from around the room. We pull apart and Lizzie steps behind me in embarrassment.

"Everyone; I'd like you to meet Lizzie Kentis. Lizzie this is everyone." I laugh knowing this isn't exactly how I had planned everyone meeting the love of my life but it is what it is.

"Hi." She waves.

"There's our Lizzie. I'm so glad you could make it!" I hear Mom come from the middle of the crowd. She wraps Lizzie up in her arms and Lizzie smiles.

"I'm so glad you called and invited me. I would have missed this if you hadn't." She says lifting our hands which are still holding the other.

"Oh I'm so happy you two finally told each other how you felt. I've wanted that since I first met you Lizzie. I could tell my boy here was head over heels in love with you at that first meeting."

"Well I wish I would have known!" Lizzie laughs and winks at me.

"Everything happens in God's time, my dear." Mom says, takes Arianna from Lizzie's arms and wanders off into the throng of people standing around.

"This is a well-attended party man." Tarley says reminding me that he's also still standing here.

"Yes when my sister asks people to show up, they do. This town is full of caring individuals that want to see the best happen for everyone. You'll soon see that." I pat him on the shoulder.

"It's beginning to grow on me. And if that beauty over there would give me the time of day it'll be even better." He points towards a brunette standing near Aaron and I immediately smile knowing he doesn't have a chance.

"That's Monica and you'll strike out every time. Just ask Carter over there that's standing right by her looking like a love sick puppy."

"You're one to be talking." He motions to Lizzie making her blush.

"At least she talks to me. Monica will barely even say a word to him. According to Aaron he's been trying since she moved here."

"Well maybe she just hadn't met the right one yet." Tarley heads of to have a word with the elusive Monica.

"This should be good." I say to Lizzie and kiss her temple. "Ready to meet everyone else?"

"There's a lot more to meet isn't there?" She bugs her eyes out at the thought.

"Yes babe there is but they're all great people."

"If they're anything like you then they'll be amazing." She raises up and kisses my lips right in front of everyone and I can't help but think about things I shouldn't be thinking of.

"You must be Lizzie? We've heard a lot about you. Glad you could join us." Aaron says as he and Amie stop in front of us.

"Yes, it's great to be here. You've got a great family I hear." Lizzie says and smiles. Already turning on that charm.

"You'll meet them all by the end of the night I'm sure. But I'm the best Blake brother there is. And this is my wife Amie." Lizzie and Amie return smiles to each other.

"And I'm the best Blake brother there is." We all laugh as Austin comes strutting in front of Aaron.

"Oh well that title is sure getting thrown around a lot tonight." Lizzie brings laughter from everyone. I feel nothing but pride knowing she's going to fit in just perfect with everyone here in Colvin.

"And I'm Leah his wife and this is Adalynn." Lizzie leans down and touches the baby's nose.

"She is just precious. Congratulations."

"We should let others have their time with you but it was great to meet you Lizzie. Come by the nursery anytime." Leah says as she ushers Austin away from us.

"Didn't you say there was a sister too? And where is your brother-in-law?" Lizzie looks at me confused; having a hard time keeping everyone straight.

"There's a lot of people to get straight. You don't have to remember them all tonight babe."

"I'm good with names, just not until I have faces to go with."

"Aiden is probably in the kitchen with Karlie doing something inappropriate. Let's go see and break it up." I shake my head knowing that's exactly what we're going to walk in on. Lizzie giggles as we go.

36

Hours later I'm standing here thinking about how there are so many people here that it's kind of overwhelming. But they're all so great. I could really see myself living here. Wait. What? You could see yourself living here in Colvin? Hmmmm.

"Are you ready to go love?" Jonathan finds me while I'm talking to his Mom in another room.

"Where is Arianna? Is she ready to leave Aleah?" I ask knowing she's going to be upset to leave her cousin.

"Actually Karlie's going to keep her tonight so we can have some time alone." Jonathan says and wiggles his eyebrows.

"I see. Well, I am kinda tired and could use a hot bath. Could you take me back to your house so I can get my car?"

"I can do that. Let's go." He says without arguing the fact that he wants to go with me. I'll play this until he does I guess.

Once we get to his Mom's house he gets out of the car and comes around to open mine. He gives me a big wet kiss before shutting my door.

"Thanks for the ride Jonathan. I'll come by tomorrow before I leave for the airport." I say and start to walk to the rental car parked at the curb. I don't hear him say a word and when I turn around to say something to him I realize he's not there.

"Um where are you?" I seriously can't see him anywhere.

He pops into view coming from the front door at a dead run. With a bag in his hand.

"Ready to go?"

"You're going with me?"

"You think I'm going to let you be in this town and out of my sight tonight?" He smiles and gets into the passenger seat of the car without another word. Well then that's settled. I smile in anticipation of what's to come.

"This place is beautiful." He says once we walk in the front doors of the B&B.

"You should see the garden. I could sit in it painting for weeks."

"Show me?" He takes my hand and raises his eyebrows in question.

"Of course. I'm sure they have lights." We walk to the garden and it takes my breath away to see it at night too.

"Wow this is amazing Lizzie. I can see lots of pieces from all of this." He sits on the bench and pulls me onto his lap.

"I could put my easel over in that corner and paint that. Then over there it could be so I could paint that. I would have a whole gallery of paintings before I could stop." I look down at Jonathan to find that he's gazing up at me with the most loving look on his face.

"I love you Lizzie. I love you so much it hurts." He puts his hand around the back of my neck and pulls me down to his lips.

"I love you too Jonathan and I was so afraid you didn't feel the same about me and wouldn't want me here." I say and look down at my hands. He puts a finger under my chin and raises my head to his eyes.

"I will forever want you here Lizzie. Nothing would make me happier than to have you here all the time. But is that something you would want to do?"

"Actually I have nothing to go back to. All of my stuff is sitting in boxes right inside Zandra's apartment."

"Did he kick you out or did you move out?"

"Zandra made me see that I didn't belong there or with him. She showed me that I belong here with you and Arianna." I lean down and kiss him lightly.

"Will you move here then? You could stay with me and Arianna at Mom's house until we can figure out where we want to live."

"Are you sure your Mom would want you, Arianna, Tarley and myself to be living with her?" I laugh.

"Well, we could always do it temporarily until everyone figures things out. I know I can't let you go again. Even if we have to rent a room here for a while."

"I don't want to be away from you two either. It killed me when you left before. I think I was lost without both of you. I tried telling myself it was just Arianna that I missed so drastically but it was both of you."

"Never again. I'll fly back with you tomorrow and we'll pack your stuff up and drive my pickup back here."

"What about Arianna?"

"Mom and Karlie will keep her until we get back. I know they'll be happy if you're coming home with me."

"That sounds like Heaven Jonathan. I want nothing more than to be with you and Arianna forever. I really do love you." I kiss him again with a heart overflowing with love.

"We had better get inside. I'm having a very hard time keeping my hands to myself. I've wanted to touch you and make love to you for so long Lizzie."

"I've felt the same way. Take me inside and love me Jonathan." I stand up only to have Jonathan put an arm behind my knees and one behind my back as he carries me into the B&B to my room.

I have never been happier in my entire life. This man is the best thing to happen to me and that little girl of his is my whole world.

Thank you Marianna for bringing him to us. I know you did all of this and I will forever be grateful to you. Love you sister. You can rest in peace now knowing Arianna and I are where we belong.

Epilogue

Monica looks like an angel tonight at Karlie's party. I can't take my eyes off her. Her hair's pinned up with little sparkly things that I couldn't name if I tried. Her dress is the color of the ocean and those eyes are sparkling just like the stars in the sky. And those legs, don't get me started on those legs. Wow.

How am I ever going to get this beautiful woman to go out with me? I've tried everything I can think of and she shoots me down.

I saw the buddy of Jonathan Doone's looking at her earlier and I'll probably break his face if he comes to talk to her. Not that she'll give him the time of day either.

I just don't get why she keeps saying no. I've never had this issue before with women. They're usually lined up wanting me before I get around to asking them. That makes me want Monica even more. Must be all about the chase; wanting what I can't have.

Aaron tells me to be patient and he should know since he's known her for so long but good grief I've been patient for a long time.

Maybe she really doesn't like me. Maybe I'm revolting to her? No way. Never happened before why would it now?

"Do you want another drink Mon?" I lean down next to her ear and ask quietly.

She leans her body away from me and simply says, "Nope."

"Suit yourself sweet cheeks." I'll go get my own drink. Or two. Grrrr. That woman is infuriating.

***

I don't know how much longer I can keep my irritation under

control when it comes to the player over there. Carter hasn't stopped trying to get me to go out with him since I met him. I don't know how else I'm supposed to turn him down without compromising our jobs.

Yes, Aaron thinks it's hilarious that he's so obsessed with me but I don't. I am a woman in a man's world and I don't want them all looking at me any differently than they do already.

I don't wear tight clothes, I don't wear makeup and I don't flirt. So why won't he get the hint? If he didn't work for Aaron I might actually say yes, but not while he's on the payroll for Double B.

"Do you want another drink Mon?" I hear him whisper in my ear from behind. My first instinct is to lean into him but I have to fight that so I lean away. And when he calls me sweet cheeks I want to shove my fist down his throat. What kind of man calls a woman that these days? Only ones who think women belong at home with the kids. Not this girl.

Oh and who is this hot male specimen coming towards me? He's a sight for sore eyes. He's not coming to talk to me though, probably the bimbos in the corner with all the cleavage on full display.

I look around me to see who he could be approaching to find no one is around me. I look back at him and he's smiling at me and definitely coming my way. Holy heck what do I do now?

"Hi. My name is Tarley. I'm told your name is Monica?" He simply says. No big come on? No chauvinistic words or rehearsed pickup lines? Interesting.

"Yes, you're correct. Nice to meet you Tarley. That's an interesting name." I reach my hand out for a shake but he only holds both of mine in between his.

"It's great to meet you. I wasn't sure if your boyfriend would allow me to talk to you though." He smiles making butterflies take flight inside me.

"I don't have a boyfriend but you're probably referring to Carter. He won't get the hint that I'm not interested." I know I'm frowning and I really don't want to be doing that with this sexy man standing in front of me.

"Then I say we go find somewhere to talk and maybe that'll help get the point across?" He lifts an eyebrow in question and I can't help but need a breath before I can say another word.

"I think that might actually do the trick. Or at least nudge it in the right direction." I stand and am surprised when he takes my hand in his and leads the way to the outdoor patio that just so happens to have a free table and two chairs. How perfect.

***

"Where the heck did she go? I was gone two minutes and now she's gone." I start to zig zag my way through the crowd in search of my princess when I step around the corner of the living room and stop dead in my tracks. What the heck?

I see through the sliding glass doors that Monica has been joined at a table outside by none other than the guy I didn't think was a threat. How did he get her to smile and laugh like that? This is not cool.

"Your face is turning red Carter. Might want to close your mouth too before you start to drool." My best friend Maysen says and pats me on the back.

"What the heck am I seeing here? I can't even get her to talk to me let alone laugh with me." I spit out getting angrier by the second.

"Dude, she must not be into you. And they're only talking. It's not like they're leaving together or hooking up."

"Oh, do not even go there if you value your tongue and pretty face."

"My wife values those things more than I do." He smiles making me want to throw up. All these happy go lucky couples around this place seem to be everywhere I turn. And my girl is outside flirting with another man! In front of me and the whole world to see!

"I don't know what else to do about her."

"Maybe it's time to move on Carter. You've made a fool out of yourself enough haven't you?" I hear Aaron say as he joins Maysen and I.

"Well I just don't get it. I've never had trouble getting a woman to go on a date with me!" I yell getting very upset.

"Calm down man you're making a scene. That's definitely not the way to win her over." Maysen says and ushers me into another room.

"You should really move on and if she thinks you're not interested anymore she might change her mind. Or you'll find someone more suited for you." Aaron says but I take complete offense to that statement.

"More suited for me? What the heck is that supposed to mean?" Maysen rolls his eyes at this outburst.

"Dude, you've had too much to drink and I'm taking you home before Karlie and Aiden kick you out." Aaron nods at Maysen and my night is quickly cut short.

"Fine this party blows anyway." I look one last time towards Monica and the big guy in disgust. "I guess he can have her."

***

"It has been so great to laugh with someone who isn't shooting off crude remarks left and right. Men just aren't made like you anymore." I say to Tarley truly meaning it. I've had a great time talking to him tonight.

"So you really don't like this Carter guy?"

"I don't like the player in him and I don't like being treated like a piece of meat. I've worked very hard to survive in a man's world at work and I'm not about to ruin it by dating one of the crew members."

"So if he changed all of that you'd give him a chance?"

"Are you trying to set me up with him or what?"

"No. Just curious about what you do like in men."

"To be honest, I'm really liking everything about you right now. But I just met you and this chat is as far as it's going to go tonight."

"Couldn't have said it better myself. Can I walk you to your car?"

"Please. And thank you again for keeping me company tonight. I always feel awkward around here being the newbie and not being a Blake or Doone."

"If I've learned anything this weekend it's that being a part of this big community is like having family. They don't care what your last name is."

"I guess you're right. I've been worrying so much about how

everyone perceives me that I haven't tried to get to know the people here. Until you. Thank you again Tarley." I lean up and kiss his cheek knowing this is the beginning of a beautiful friendship. Or more? Who knows; don't rush it Monica.

"Friends?" He asks as we walk to my car.

"Most definitely. Does this mean you're sticking around awhile?"

"I believe I am. Not sure where I'm going to live since Lizzie came to town to be with Jonathan and Arianna but I think I will stay in town."

"Well, until next time it was awesome spending time with you. We should do it again sometime."

"Sometime soon I hope." He smiles and walks back to the party.

"Hey! Did you need a ride? I think I saw Jonathan and Lizzie sneak off earlier."

"You know what I think you're right. Would you mind?"

"Of course not. Hop in. My car's a little messy because I work out of it a lot more than I do my office." I can't believe I'm letting this big man crawl into my messy car. How embarrassing.

"I don't mind at all. I don't even have a car anymore so you're one step ahead of me." He smiles but looks away quickly. There's a lot more to this man that meets the eye.

"Well, I hope one day you'll tell me your story since I all but rattled my entire life story off to you tonight." We both laugh.

"It was great getting to know you. I'm just a tougher nut to crack. But you've got a great start. Thanks for the ride. See you soon."

He leans over and kisses my cheek. Heat rushes up my body and straight to my face as he exits my car with a grin as wide as his face. He just kissed my cheek and I'm blushing. What has gotten into me?

***

"Mayse do you think she's ever going to give me a chance?"

"Carter I really don't think so. You need to move on and find someone else."

"But I don't want to find someone else. I love her Maysen."

"Love her? How? You said she's barely even spoken to you!"

"Why is that so hard to believe?"

"You don't even know her Carter. How can you love her?"

"I know she tries to dress down at work so none of us treat her differently than we do Aaron, I know she has eyes that sparkle like stars, I know she loves warm cinnamon rolls, I know she works very hard and loves her job."

"Wow you know a lot more about her than I thought you did."

"I am observant when it comes to her."

"Or just a stalker? You're kinda scaring me here dude."

"Maysen, when you first saw Audrey you knew she was the one for you didn't you?"

"Yes, but I didn't think I would ever see her again."

"I see Monica six days a week so have a little faith in me."

"You're delusional Carter."

"I'm telling you; she's the one for me."

CPSIA information can be obtained
at www.ICGtesting.com
Printed in the USA
LVHW082143210322
714046LV00028B/876

9 781519 152367